STRANGE FISH

22-03-22 Milton Schorr

STRANGE FISH

MILTON SCHORR

PILGRIM'S PRESS BOOKS
Published by Pilgrim's Press Books
28 Hof Street, Cape Town, 8001, South Africa.
info@pilgrimspressbooks.com

First published in South Africa by Pilgrim's Press Books 2021
2nd Edition

THE NATIONAL LIBRARY OF SOUTH AFRICA
Schorr, M.L, 1981
Strange Fish
ISBN 978-0-620-93267-7 (print)
978-0-620-93268-4 (e-book)

Set in 12/16pt Bodoni 72 Oldstyle

CONTENTS

Chapter One 11
Chapter Two 19
Chapter Three 28
Chapter Four 36
Chapter Five 46
Chapter Six 54
Chapter Seven 67
Chapter Eight 77
Chapter Nine 89
Chapter Ten 117
Chapter Eleven 129
Chapter Twelve 142
Chapter Thirteen 152
Chapter Fourteen 168
Chapter Fifteen 193

'All my life, my heart has yearned for a thing
I cannot name.' – André Breton

PART I

CHAPTER ONE

The boy has his line in the water, and through it he can feel everything. The gentle pull of the current below, the creaking of the kelp beds as they swirl in the green water, and the clicking of the *kray* as they tiptoe their way over rock and shell, hungry.

The surface glitters. He closes his eyes against the glare. Here in the northern channel, between the outer rocks of the Island, all is feel but for the slapping water against the hull of the little boat. All is the line.

Around his bare feet five fish lie, four of them *spookvis*, ghost-grey and flat and blunt. They stare, eyes sightless mirrors to the sky, while the fifth, a strange one, continues to gasp. The boy looks at it, scowling. The fish is grey also, but there is a shimmer between its scales: a rainbow rippling in the rain. He has not seen such a fish before. It lies quiet, its gills fanning the empty air.

'Strange fish,' he mutters into his sparse beard.

He turns from his catch to the sea. The Sentinel rises above him, a ten-foot tower of black rock marking the edge of the island cluster that he has known always. Beneath it, on the green water, a tiny white V trails from his line. He allows his eyes to relax, the V melting into the clouded water. Once again he feels down, all of his attention diving to the hook and its meat, and through it, searching for a sign.

The ocean breathes.

Something plays in him, a flitting in his stomach, a tightening.

The line falls from his finger.

The corner of his lip tugs upward, ever so slightly.

There.

A slow pull and then nothing. But it is enough.

Twee faam – two fathoms – beneath him a *spookvis* has the bait in its sucking mouth. He can see the little fish in his mind's eye. Tasting quietly, eyes open as the pleasure of the wet meat seeps through. Inside the bait is the hook, but the fish does not know it.

'*Eat*,' he murmurs.

'*Eat*,' agrees the fish.

He knows his quarry is still testing, tasting. When the line begins a longer pull, so slight that only instinct will show it, he will know the fish has begun to turn and swim. Then he will strike.

He watches the line, listening, waiting.

A chill runs through him. He looks up to the horizon. A bank of white is laid out, reaching from the sea halfway to the midmorning sun.

He frowns, looking back down at the fish between his feet.

Only five.

The fog is moving at speed. When it hits the fish will dive away and there will be nothing for it but the slow way home, watching for the Island's rocks rising from the gloom.

His eyes return to the water and his ears to the gentle creak of the line on his finger. There it is. That pulling, lighter than air, that slow pressure of a sucking mouth.

'*Eat*,' he murmurs, raising his eyes to the approaching fog.

'*Eat*,' hums the little fish.

Bang! The line razors through the green water, his rubber-covered fingers curling as it cuts the little one below.

Swish-swish, swish-swish, he hauls the fish in, his arms slapping against his rubber-suited sides, the glistening coils of the line gathering at his feet.

There it is! That faint silver in the green, a flashing disk down there. He pulls, now seeing the tail, the fin, and the eye, as it comes fighting to the surface with the hook in its mouth.

The creature bulges beneath the veil, magnified, until he reaches down and takes the line in a turn around his wrist and plucks it from the water. He swings it clear and lets it slap down on the thwart, criss-crossed with the years of his knife. Another *spookvis*, as grey and flat as the others. He lays a hand to its gasping and twists the hook from its throat. It falls to the bottom and sets to dancing against the smothering air, as quickly he turns to his motor and jerks it to life.

He swings the boat in an arc beneath the Sentinel, setting his bow to home.

'Only six.' The words drip though his mind as he speeds across the water. 'Only six.'

Five are *spookvis*, the last still wet and kicking. But the sixth is different, a strange colour pulsing through its flesh. It lives still, one eye watching the fading sun.

Hours later the fog has burned away and the little town of the Baai shimmers in the summer heat. The boy makes his way along a rutted track through the veld. He pulls against his cart. With only six in the bed the frame is heavier than the load. The cart's wooden wheels dig into the sand; his dusty toes dig in also. The sand is hot between them.

'Just six,' he mutters through his twisted lip. It would have been easier to carry them, but the cart had to be taken home anyway.

The smell comes first: a blend of salt, and fish, and diesel. And now he sees it. Ahead of him rises the *fabriek* – the factory – a rash of low buildings clustered near the water, not far from the high-tide mark. The old jetty stands rotten among the rocks and the lapping sea, unused for twenty years since the trucks and the highway came.

He winds his way between the low fynbos – hardy plants built for drought, and salt, and sun. He leans against the weight of the cart as he crosses the boundary line. The sand lies soft and thick in a bank here, a jerk to pull it over, and then the wheels take to concrete and the cart lightens. It clatters behind him.

He stops to let a forklift pass; it whirs on its electric wheels with a crate of salted *harder* held high, and then on he goes, into the shadow of the open sorting floor.

A row of women are cleaning and filleting a meagre catch of *harder* for the salt racks. Thin fingers of fish slip down the line and through their deft hands. He keeps his head low, his eyes on the ragged floor. He knows they see him. All of them, looking at the one pulling his cart, who would call himself a fisherman. Through his brows he looks up and to his left. There is the office above the factory floor. The door is ajar; he marks that. His knuckles tighten on his pull bar. An open door means one thing: the owner of the *fabriek* is here.

The big weighing scale lies ahead of him. Once he has logged his catch he will be able to leave. He begins to hurry.

'And, how goes?'

The boy stops, caught. It is Salie the storeman who has spoken; Salie, the keeper of the scale.

He does not answer. Instead he merely nods while keeping his eyes to his bare feet.

'*Is die chokkie leeg?* – Is the cart empty?' asks Salie, walking up and peering into it, his notebook and pencil in hand.

The boy does not respond. He stands stoop-shouldered, the yoke of the cart hanging loose across his chest.

'And the sea?'

'Nothing good,' whispers the boy.

'Hell now!' Salie gives a short whistle and taps the side of the cart. 'Look at that!'

The boy scowls, his eyes fixed to his feet.

'Jonny, you got a rainbow fish!'

'A rainbow fish?'

'That's a good fish,' says Salie, reaching down to prod the shimmering creature. 'Hell, look! It's still breathing!'

The boy peers into his cart. In the bottom lie his five *spookvis*, dead. But the sixth... Its gills fan the empty air while its eye looks up to them. To the boy it seems to see them and see beyond them.

'Rainbow fish. That's a good eating fish.' Salie leans in close to the boy, speaking low. 'You want to trade it? I'll give you a pallet of harder...' Salie nods to the women, their hands raking fish, and then he glances up to the office with its door ajar. 'Your weight will look much better.'

The boy studies the bright fish. He shakes his head and instead reaches down to scoop it up. He opens his tuck box fixed to the front of the cart and slips it in.

Salie shrugs. 'It's a good eating fish, you will have a good supper tonight.' The store-man claps the boy's shoulder and smiles into his eyes. Old Salie. The boy knows this face well. He is about to return the smile, when Salie frowns.

'Watch out,' he whispers.

The boy turns to look. In the bustle of the sorting floor a man is lumbering towards them. He is dressed in the clothes of the men of means of the Baai – big felt-lined boots, tiny denim shorts, a khaki shirt and a leather wide-brimmed hat, but that is where the similarity ends. He towers over the folk of the sorting floor. His boots are twice the size of their own, his head and shoulders loom above them, and despite his size he moves with an alarming grace. The women go quiet as Uncle Mike Morkel, MD of the Hansbaai Fishing Consortium stalks down the line, a bear in shorts and shirt.

'Jonny. How goes it?' Rumbles the giant as he reaches the two of them. He drops his large and hairy hand onto the cart, rocking it. 'How was the day?'

The boy does not answer.

'He has some *spookvis*,' says Salie.

The huge man peers into the cart, his sharp brown eyes looking down at the five lying dead there.

'The fog came in,' whispers the boy into his wispy beard. 'I went all the way out to the point, before sun-up.'

'The catch is very shit,' says Salie, nodding.

Uncle Mike nods also, placing a massive hand between the boy's shoulder blades, letting the warmth of his great palm seep into the bones.

'Five *spookvis*. This is your worst catch yet.' The big man sighs. 'How am I going to feed everyone?'

The boy stares at his bare feet. Scales are crusted between his toes. 'I will try the reef tomorrow,' he whispers. 'Maybe I'll have some luck.'

Uncle Mike nods, and then turns his gaze back to the five fish.

'A poor size. Weigh them, and come back to me tomorrow.'

'I'll need some petrol,' whispers the boy. 'The reef is far.'

'No petrol. You can't expect petrol when you bring me this.'

There is a brief pressure from the hand on his shoulder, a pressure that creaks the bones. The boy freezes, waiting, hoping, and then the pressure is gone. He turns to look, and there is the great figure of Uncle Mike striding from them, his body rising to the angular gallows of his shoulders. The boy sighs, the dread in his stomach passing as the big man climbs the steps to the office and stoops as he steps inside. Salie raises a hand to pat the boy's shoulder.

'The fish were not biting.'

'Nobody caught good today.'

Salie reaches into the cart and pulls out the inner crate, dumping the five spookvis onto the scale. The needle on the dial barely flickers, and Salie jots their weight down.

'I tried. It's the sea.'

Salie flicks the fish one by one onto the vlekking line.

'Could I get some petrol for tomorrow, Salie? The reef is far.'

Salie glances up at the office, the door ajar. 'I'm sorry, *seun* – my boy. He will know.'

'But how much did others catch?'

'You can't expect petrol when you bring only five.'

'But did anyone else catch?'

Again Salie glances up to the office with the door ajar before flicking his eyes to the boy. 'No,' he mouths, before turning back to his paper.

'Come on, Salie, from the back store,' whispers the boy, reaching out to tug at the man's sleeve. Gently, Salie pulls it away.

'Enjoy your rainbow fish. It's a good eating fish.'

The boy sighs. He turns his cart, his eyes to the concrete of the sorting floor, and then he heads home.

The boy's hut stands by the side of the track, full of roof and window and door. Before the dilapidated building is a patch of sand that once contained grass, and around that is a sagging fence and a rusting gate. Behind it an apple tree rises, its leaves sparse in the summer heat. He lets go of his cart to rest under the old, patched awning. He unclips the tuck box, feeling the weight of the rainbow fish inside, and clicks through the rusted gate.

'At least I have supper.'

He places the tuck box on the rough table outside and pulls his cutting board near. In the sparse rains of summer he prefers to cook outside and sometimes even to sleep, wondering up at the stars.

He takes his knife from its sheath and runs it across his thigh, cleaning the blood-flecked blade. With his other hand he unhooks the clasp of the tuck box and reaches inside, bringing the rainbow fish out into the light.

He places it on the table, and his blade pauses in the air.

Still, the fish is breathing. As air wafts across its ribboned gills, the little fish looks up at him.

'Strange,' thinks the boy.

'*Eat?*' he asks the little fish.

It does not answer.

He peers at the thing and sees that in its flesh there is more to be discovered: a sheen between the scales. He shifts the cutting board towards the sun. The fish comes alive, flapping in the light, its flesh filled with the colours of the sky and sea, shimmering from tail to gill.

'What are you?' asks the boy as he traps the fish with a gentle hand and brings it back to the cutting board. He places his palm on its flank, quieting it with his own quiet.

He slips his blade beneath the jaw of the little fish and pulls it through to the tail.

He pushes the mess of intestine, lung, heart, liver and bowel aside and cuts across the tail and beneath the gills, opening the fish up to the sky. He takes it by the tail and dunks it in a bucket of sea water standing ready, cleaning it, and then he dumps the guts in the bucket also. Bait for tomorrow.

He leaves the little fish filleted, placed beneath a net to ward off the flies, then he collects fresh water from his two big drums round the side of his hut and returns to wash down the cart. With a tattered sack he scrapes it clean of scales and blood, and then he douses the sack in fresh water and leaves them to dry in the afternoon sun, placing his freshly washed knife beside them. He climbs from his torn trousers and his tattered shirt and douses them also. Naked, he returns to the side of his shelter, where the fynbos comes creeping down from the hills, and washes his blood-caked hands before once again putting them in the clean water and washing his body. Finally clean, he lies down to rest on his mat within his hut, away from the still burning sun.

He dreams of the deep.

Later, his appetite takes him back to the fish, and he lights a fire beneath the blaze of the Milky Way. He grills the little fish and eats it, looking up to the stars. He turns his attention to the remains, scooping them out of the water. And then he pauses. Among the soft organs of the fish is something hard. He turns to light his gas lamp, and by its hissing white light he sees it: almost round, and flickering with all the colours of the fish itself. A pearl.

He plucks it from the mess in his hand and rolls it in the centre of his palm.

He lays his eye to it.

In it, the future dances.

The boy smiles.

Beneath the table, amidst the muck of its guts, the head of the fish lies still, its dead eye looking up to the moon.

CHAPTER TWO

S*lip-slip, slip-slip* go his oars as he dips them in dawn's water.

Thank-you-thank-you, thank-you-thank-you sounds his mind as he pulls the oars towards him, the handles worn by generations of fishermen, and then pushes them away so that the blades swing out, streaming cold.

In the east there is pink on the water.

'*Thank-you-thank-you, thank-you-thank-you.*'

On the transom, on a pad of old and frayed fish *meel* sacking, is his pearl.

'*Thank-you-thank-you, thank-you-thank-you.*'

The sun is above the ocean when he throws out his anchor and it bubbles down to the seabed of the northern channel, only three *faam* deep. The water is clear today, the green of yesterday replaced by the sharp grey of the seabed, the brown kelp and crowds of colourful anemone. He peers over the lip of his little boat, looking through the veil left and right.

He will not see the fish, their thin silhouettes are hidden unless they turn and allow the sun to light them. But it is the shell beds he's after, mussel clusters that are a wash of black near the tideline, the perlemoen beds a brush of mottled white deeper down, clinging to the low rocks, and deeper still, hiding, sheltered by overhangs, the clam beds, the pearl beds, where he will find his bounty.

He pauses in his looking. A shadow flits across the sand, gliding and turning.

'*Eat*,' murmurs the boy, a smile on his lips.

The sea lion turns on her back to look up at him, flashing her dog-teeth.

'*Eat*,' she grins, and then glides away.

His smile turns to a frown. Out here, just north of the Island, where the continental shelf drops off to the deep ocean only a boat's length away, there are predators also. Many times he has seen a sea lion awash in the shallows, half of it bitten away, and once he saw a man reach down to scoop up a *spookvis* that had slipped the hook and lain just beneath the surface, exhausted, and pull his wrist from the water trailing flesh and bone.

He shakes the thought away and stands up to let the new sun touch his body. He pulls off his old jersey. He flexes his arms, raising them high, lacing and unlacing his fingers, stretching all of himself as he once again looks down, scanning the ocean floor.

There, at the entrance to the channel coming in from the deep ocean, just beneath the rising finger of the Sentinel, a dark smudge on the sea floor. A clam bed, he thinks, obscured by the trailing kelp above it. Once again he lets the sun touch him, because down there it will be cold. He takes up his mask and places it over his eyes. He takes up his knife and clamps it between his teeth, and then he slips into the water. He treads there a moment, gulping his final breath, and then he dives.

Cold. It encases his body. *Cold.* A lens through which to see.

Swiftly he swims down to the point where rock meets bottom at the base of the Sentinel. Life springs up to meet him.

What was an orange smudge above is now a giant anemone, its fingers trailing, and spiked purple anemones, and thick and fleshy kelp rising from their anchor to find the sun. He swims strongly. He does not like being in the water. He remembers the one-handed man's scream.

Shivers wash through him as he kicks down and down, letting the pressure run through his throat and out through his ears. The drop off to the left is clearer now, the vast deep out there, the emptiness of it causing panic to rise in him. The smudge he saw from the surface crystallises into clean black rock, a perfect overhang. He kicks toward it.

And then his stroke stalls.

A flicker just outside his vision.

He twists round to study the bright jumble of the channel, fear directing his hand to the blade between his teeth. Behind him the open ocean yawns, and the nerves in his back dance.

Again he kicks down, and for the first time he feels the urge to breathe.

The cold crushes down on him. The sun is so far away.

Closer to the base now, he can see a smear of pink in the shadow, just as he had hoped. He smiles. Pink is the colour of clam.

And then again there is that flash on the edge of his sight. He spins to look, the whole world revolving with his turn.

Nothing but the clear cold.

He clenches his teeth now, the first convulsion pulsing through him. He has a minute left, he knows. Just enough time to make sure.

The bed comes up to meet him. It is larger than he thought, and deeper – a tunnel into the rising rock. He hangs there on the edge of the shelf, peering in.

A carpet of black mussel covers the mouth and sides, but deeper in he sees what he's looking for. He reaches in, wanting to touch and confirm the lip of the clam before he takes his blade and shucks it from the rock and rises with it to the surface, and the sun. His fingers almost brush it. And then blue pulses within the black before him, and he realises his mistake. These are not the shelled rows of a clam bed. Before he can jerk his hand free, a black finger lays itself across his wrist.

Adrenalin explodes, he needs to rip his hand away, but the black convulses again, and this time a disc opens before him. The mollusk's eye regards him, and its finger tightens.

'*Eat*,' says the giant octopus.

He pulls, jerking from spine to hand, kicking his legs up and into the rock. Every movement reveals a new black finger with a power he cannot fight. Bubbles stream from his mouth. The cold crowds in on him, freezing his eyes, streaming down his throat. The great strength tightens, and again, convulsing, pulling him into the tunnel.

Above him a school of *spookvis* turn, slivers of dark against his little boat drifting on the surface, and beyond it the bright sun. Life begins to leave him. In a rush he understands: His time was brief, all his days are gone, and this was always to be. '*Thank you, thank you,*' mutters the boy, the words plopping from his mouth into a final bubble. 'Thank you.'

As his mind is enfolded in the slow peace of forgetting, he sees that flitting shadow again. It is rushing towards him, straight from the vast emptiness. Its impact shakes him, his synapses fire for the final time. All is confusion, for instead of the black eye of a shark here is a green one, a clear eye the colour of the water looking straight at him, and then he is gone.

He wakes to the sound of dripping water. He is desperately cold. He can feel rock at his back; his arms are numb. He opens his eyes. Above him faint sunlight dances through a hole in the rock. Where is he? Only his face is above the surface. All around him is the cold.

'*What are you looking for?*'

The voice is inside him. It is the voice of fishes. He looks about him. But all is gloom.

'*What are you looking for?*'

Just like the fish, the words begin as a feeling peeling through him, but unlike them these words are clear, and directed at him. He feels heat in his foot. Something has touched him, a long finger like that of the octopus. It burns, and he jerks his foot away.

Laughter. It chimes, soft, like the distant church bell on Sundays when he walks in the fields. There is a mind in the water with him.

'You don't want to eat me?' he asks the gloom.

'*You are too big for me to eat.*'

The boy remembers the power of the animal as it dragged him into the tunnel. Perhaps this is its cave. But this voice cannot be that of the monster. This voice is laughter.

'*How can you speak?*'

Again, that laughter.

'How can you hear?'

Again he feels the heat upon his foot, that whisper of a limb brushing over his. He does not look into the dark water lest he see horror there.

'I just listen,' he says, this time speaking in the way of fish that only he knows.

'Come to me.'

He leans forward, wanting to, but he is afraid.

'What are you looking for?' The voice is playful, tugging at his heart.

'A pearl.'

He puts his eyes to the water. Immediately she is there, her eyes just a finger from his own. They are green, flecked with all the colours of the seabed, and they look straight into his soul.

'Are you looking for this?' Her hand appears, fingers tapered and unfolding around a bone white palm. In its centre is a pearl just like his own.

'How did you find it?'

'It's mine.'

'I have one also.' He slips further into the water, forgetting about the sun. *'It's on my boat.'*

'What is a boat?'

Both hang in the water, suspended between the above and the below.

'I know you.'

She nods, her eyes bright in the cold.

She laughs, bubbles streaming from her mouth.

He laughs too, and reaches his hand out to hers. *'I have heard you before. I have heard you many times, laughing among the fishes.'*

'Why are you looking for a pearl?'

His eyes are dark and they pierce her through the water. *'So that I can be free.'*

He reaches out his fingers, scarred from the line, and she extends her own. Their palms touch, the pearl between them. Again he laughs and the first bubbles of his new life plop from his mouth. They rise to the faraway sun.

Suddenly her fingers tighten around his and she pulls him all the way under.

'Wait!'

But she does not listen. With frightening strength she hauls him into the deep.

In a rush they pass the opening of the cave. '*Eat*,' he hears a growl from the curling creature there.

'*Eat*,' he replies, but they are already gone. The northern channel is behind them and below the bottom has dropped off to fifty *faam*, a hundred, an endless blue ahead, and together they rush into it.

Seven nautical miles out seagulls swirl. Below them five ships are at anchor, their lines let out to a hundred and forty-two *faam*. These ships are bright with metal, bristling with satellite dishes, and are far from their native shores. On them strange men sit attentive, cloth across their faces against the bright sun, rubber about their bodies, and on their fingers more rubber, and their white lines cut sharp as they pull tuna from the deep.

The ships have hit it right, lying across and above one of the great summer schools. The men work at speed, dropping their lines. The *dollies*, the painted lures in silver, red, and neon blue, fall in graceful arcs before being whipped back. They trail upwards through the blue, their hooks spinning, and the tuna rise behind them, open-mouthed, and themselves go spinning to eternity.

Blood from the gaffs leaks into the water, trailing in clouds as the tuna break through, and the *dollies* plop through the red fog like bullets.

Beneath the spinning lines she and he dance, thirty *faam* deep, deeper than he has ever dived, as around them the tuna rise.

'*Eat...*' she hums as the fish surge, her voice swirling in his mind.

'*Eat*,' he breathes, bubbles streaming from his mouth.

'*Eat*,' rumbles the great circling school, bunching up and then bunching down as the *dollies* spin the rays of the distant sun.

She takes his hand then and drags him down. The light fades as they sink, and the bodies of the fish press in around them.

'*Eat*,' these larger tuna moan, slowly circling in the half-light.

Further down she pulls him, to where the light is gone and the bodies of fish have grown monstrous, festooned with light.

'*Eat*,' moans the school down there, unmoved by the plopping of the *dollies* and the spinning of the young so very high above.

A fish in the dark rears, a yawning mouth and endless teeth and a soundless clash as it cuts another in two, and two more eat the head, snapping it away before the light of it is dispersed, and there is nothing but blood in the water and bodies in the dark.

And then a new sound runs through the deep.

'*Hmm*,' it sings, a vibration growing until the water around them shakes and a giant eye passes.

'*Hmm*.' An ageless sweep of its tail takes it away, back into the black.

She laughs, her eyes alive with the ocean's secrets.

'*Eat*,' pounds the school.

'*They are turning*,' he thinks, as the pattern of their one thought pulses anew. '*They will dive*.'

She nods and spreads her arms while the water surges around them, and the school turns, and suddenly is gone.

Quickly she takes his hand and together they rise. On the surface the *dollies* spin aimlessly as the men continue to haul them aboard, wishing the tuna to return.

She taps him on his cheek, her finger like fire on his skin. Then, with a flick of her tail she darts forward, up through the water with hand outstretched, and she clasps one of the spinning *dollies* and turns with it so that the line cuts through the water, and then snaps. Empty, it skitters up to the great shadow floating above.

She takes his hand, and they leave the five ships far behind.

Above a man curses, clutching his hand to his chest. The finger throbs, blood leaking from the gash where the line slashed clean through the rubber and into bone.

'A giant fish,' he says to his fellows, 'a giant!'

He pulls the cloth away, and his face is foreign, his dark eyes slitted against the sun.

There are no more tuna. The men stow their catch, and wonder at the ways of this foreign sea.

That evening, as the earth turns from the sun, she and he swim in the open water.

'*Where are we going?*'

She stops and puts her mouth to his, filling him with air.

'*Home.*'

'*Where is home?*'

She breathes into him again, and again takes his hand, and they streak through the water, she with tail and he with feet born for this.

The pillars and columns of the Island return, so different from below.

They glide through its channels while the water turns slowly to orange.

A *shashergasse* passes them, and she reaches out and slips her fingers between the twin slits of its gills. She cradles it, turning in the translucent kingdom, holding it as it dies. She laces her finger from gill to tail, following the ridge of bone. Half of the white meat she places in her mouth, and the other she holds out to him.

'*Eat.*'

She puts the meat on his tongue.

It tastes of salt and sea. Of her.

'*It's warm down here, with you.*'

His feet hang suspended in the water, and underneath them her tail. She unfurls it, its fan spreading out until it lies flat beneath him. She brings it up to him, her fin touching his toes. She points to the surface, where only a pink glow remains.

'*Look.*'

She kicks once, raising them upward. And he sees. The same strange fish with its rainbow rippling in its scales.

'*Nightfish,*' she says.

She takes it by the belly, and the little fish relaxes in her hand. It floats with her, lulled by her touch, until she wills it and, as if waking, it waves its tail and is away into the growing night above them, swimming among the stars.

His arms open and she swims between them. He holds her, and she wraps her tail around them both.

She puts her mouth to his and breathes into his lungs.

They hang there, afire within the cold.

At dawn on a glassy sea, the boy's little boat comes gliding towards the beach. His strokes are smooth and long. The bow digs into sand. Smoothly he turns, hopping out and pulling the little boat partway out of the water. He takes two paces and falls onto the still dew-damp sand, looking out over the lightening bay.

Pink in the east.

He reaches into his pocket and pulls from it his pearl. It feels like a flame.

Again he looks out over the blue curve of the bay. Still as glass.

His smile mirrors the coming light.

The sun, when it appears, blooms in his eyes.

'Thank you. Thank you.'

CHAPTER THREE

His eyes are closed, and between the slow twirling of that red world he sees her, twirling also. Her hair is spread in a cloud about her, her green eyes are laughing into his.

He touches his finger to his lips, tastes it, and remembers the taste of her.

He sighs, and smiles.

Suddenly his body tenses.

He hears the beat of an engine circling in the morning air. His eyes snap open, above him blue sky. A shudder runs through him. He knows this sound well. He rolls to his feet and slinks into his little hut, taking his cutting board with his breakfast of fish and fruit with him. He crouches inside, beside the weathered door, waiting as the engine sound grows louder. It halts on the sandy track and spins into quiet.

'Jonothan! Jonny?'

The boy peers through a crack in the wall. He sees Uncle Mike step out of his motor. The huge man casts his eyes around the little hut with the patch of sand and the little fence, one hand on the door of his motor and a growl on his face.

'Jonny, come out here.'

The boy knows the big man will not leave. He sighs, and steps out into the sun.

'Uncle?'

'How goes it?'

'Good,' whispers the boy. He does not look at the man's face, but to the ground. 'How is it with Uncle?'

'Good. It's a nice Sunday.'

'Yes,' says the boy.

'You didn't drop your catch at the factory yesterday. Did you go out?'

The boy nods. His fire dances in the cooking pit.

'You caught nothing?'

He nods again.

Uncle Mike pushes the door of his motor closed with a click.

'There was a tuna run yesterday.' The big man takes a step toward the little hut. 'Seven miles. They caught more than all of us together.'

The boy remains rooted to the spot, his eyes come up, now fixed to the centre of the big man's chest. Uncle Mike steps through the gate. Another click as it latches behind him.

'There was nothing at the Island,' whispers the boy. 'I laid nets all day.'

'Where are your nets?'

'By the boat.' His eyes are fastened on the clear white button of the big man's khaki shirt. Helplessly, he raises them to Uncle Mike's face. 'I been on the beach.'

Uncle Mike takes a second stride towards him. 'Your nets are dry.'

Panic rises in the boy. 'I'm sorry. I didn't lay the nets. I only fished. But there was nothing.'

'Where were you?'

He cannot reply. He looks down, his eyes drawn to the dancing cooking fire.

'Sleeping in your boat. In the northern channel. Anchored all day. Salie saw you there. Sleeping all day.' The big man takes another step closer. 'Isn't that right?'

'Yes, Uncle. It's right.'

'And you ask me for petrol?'

'I'm sorry, Uncle.'

'Come here. Come closer to me.'

The boy shuffles forward.

'Come, man. Closer to me.'

Once again the boy shuffles.

The big man grabs the boy's shoulder, his fingers iron.

'Come, let me look at you.'

With his left hand Uncle Mike raises the boy's chin. The boy does not look into his eyes. *What does he see?* The boy has been told he has a gentle face, a dreamer's face. But it is marred by the cleft in his lip.

'Look at me.' The big man gives the chin a shake. The boy can no longer hide; finally, his eyes find those of Uncle Mike's. They are dark also. They promise pain.

'What are you hiding from me, Jonny? Why were you not fishing yesterday?'

'I was sleeping, Uncle. I fell asleep in my boat. I'm sorry.'

Uncle Mike begins to knead the flesh of the boy's shoulder. He works his way down, touching the skin over the triceps, feeling its fine formation, and the soft bicep, and the joint of the elbow. The boy shivers, and it frustrates the big man. *Why must he be afraid?*

'What were you doing, Jonny?'

'Nothing, Uncle. I promise.'

Uncle Mike continues to look into his eyes. The boy knows he will break, that his eyes will tell the big man what he seeks. Uncle Mike waits patiently, watching the seed of the lie drawing slowly to the surface. And he continues to knead. He is fascinated by the boy's finely drawn body, so different from the heavy bones of his own. He leaves the intricacy of the boy's hand, scarred and rough, and places his palm on the flesh of his stomach, moving sideways to the hip bone. Suddenly the eyes deliver: *panic.*

'What is it?'

'I'm sorry,' the boy whispers. 'I should have told you.'

'What is it, Jonny?'

His hand continues its exploration, onto the boy's tattered trousers, searching, feeling, rolling the rough material between his fingers.

'So.'

His eyes stay on the boy's as he slips two fingers into his pocket.

'Please...'

He withdraws his hand, something round in his palm. He holds it up to the morning sun.

'I wanted to get more before I showed you.'

The pearl sparkles. Uncle Mike studies it. It is perfect, white and shimmering blue, a living piece of the ocean.

'You found it at the Island?'

'In the Pond. A clam came up in my net. I went looking for the bed. I was diving yesterday. That is why Salie saw my boat.'

Uncle Mike closes his fist around the pearl. He slides it into his pocket.

'This goes to your debt.'

The boy nods.

'Come,' says Uncle Mike, turning to his little *bakkie* - his pickup.

The boy climbs back into his tattered pants and follows him.

The motor buzzes on the long tar road. To the east the brown veld rises to the distant mountains, and to the west and south the ocean glitters. They drive with their windows open and the hot bush-spiced wind covers them.

Uncle Mike crowds the cabin, his giant shoulders stoop over the little wheel, his left elbow thrust outward to touch the boy's chest. His goatee is dark and flecked with grey and white, and his brows bristle above his piercing eyes. His giant forearms and wrists rest on the wheel.

'Salie tells me they sat on a school for an hour. They half filled their hold, then the fish were gone.' Uncle Mike scowls at the road. 'They're sitting just outside our waters, taking our fish.'

'They got lucky,' whispers the boy. 'They use cloud-spinners. Our fish don't like cloud-spinners. The sun flashes on them.'

'Yesterday the sun came out of cloud. If they were running straight dollies, or sardine, they would have cleaned up.'

Uncle Mike casts an eye sideways at the boy. He sits slightly forward, listening, always listening. His eye wanders to his lip, hidden beneath his sparse beard. Irritation rises in him. The boy's beard irritates him. The beard is like the boy – sparse.

'I seen them at the harbour,' whispers they boy. 'I can see what they running. Anyone can see. They don't buy nothing at the harbour, not even food.'

The boy places his hands on the sun-cracked dashboard, stretching his fingers out. They are long, made to weave knots and thread hooks.

To their left the harbour slides into view. There, at anchor at the tip of the breakwater float the five foreign ships, sleek and dotted all over with antennae. Around them the local fishing fleet falls apart to the eye. Broken boats they seem, miraculously afloat, streaked with rust and the stains of old diesel.

'They stupid.' The boy shakes his shaggy head, the sound mangled by his lip. 'Shoopid.' The word whispers in the cab before the wind wipes it away.

The harbour passes. Beyond it is the factory.

Uncle Mike clicks his indicator, sliding the wheel left.

In the little parking lot the boy steps from the truck and immediately turns to the back, fishing for his filleting apron and boots.

'Not today,' says Uncle Mike, motioning for the boy to follow.

He lumbers along, passing the empty sorting line. On a Sunday the ladies are home, dozing in the church with their pastor or in the *smokkie* – the tavern – with their beer.

Uncle Mike whistles as he walks, a tune from his childhood he told the boy once, a tune from far away.

Into the maze they go, walking chipped corridors and muck-flecked walls a-hum with white fluorescents. The smell of this place is always the same. It is fish *meel*, fish bone and guts and flesh and scales ground, boiled and turned to smoke that hangs. It coats the nose. It smells of work, and money. In here are the storage units, the great fridges that in the past would smear the day's bounty with ice, freezing their eyes and fins, before they'd be boxed and sent on freighters across the globe. Today, room after room stands empty, their doors ajar, the floors scrubbed and left to dry beneath the blades of the once whirring fans, which now only creak in the wind.

Uncle Mike stops at the unit at the end of the corridor, pulling a bright, silver handle to make the rubber suck and hiss, and the big door swings open. A blast of cold greets them, and the drone of machines.

'Careful.' Uncle Mike points to the floor. The boy pauses, his bare foot hovering over ice.

'Their seas are empty.' Uncle Mike crosses the iced floor. Boxes of frozen *stokvis* rise around them. 'They learned to move far out and find the catch in open water. They can keep their catch alive for months. How do they do it?'

Uncle Mike turns to a blue plastic crate covered with a blue plastic lid. He flips the lid, revealing water.

'As a boy I lived in the cold. We had no ocean but we had rivers and lakes that would freeze over in the winter. One day a child fell through the ice. He fell in the morning and was found in the afternoon.' He nips a corner of sacking from his belt and winds it round his palm. 'When they pulled him out his body was frozen stiff. They pulled him by his arm. He was like a piece of wood.' He dips his hand into the water, drawing out an *okker*. The fish pulls against his iron fingers, contracting its long body to bring mouth to tail and then back again, gills gasping. 'We placed him beside the fire, and we rubbed him with warm towels and sang to him. He woke.'

Uncle Mike raises the twisting *okker* to his eye. 'I've been working on something,' he says, and pads to the worktable. 'Look.'

Among the tools and cables, and between discarded nuts and angled work lights, is a length of PVC pipe, hinged open. Along the edges of both halves are a series of nozzles riveted to the plastic. Inside is a smooth sheet of rubber, soft to the touch. There are clamps at either end of the pipe, as well as in the middle, waiting to clip the contraption closed.

Uncle Mike swings the *okker* into the length of the pipe and takes half a step back, his left hand dropping to a brass valve.

'Step back,' he says, moments before a blast of nitrogen covers the kicking fish. The vapour clears. The fish is rigid, its gills spread mid-breath. Uncle Mike quickly flips the pipe closed, banging the three clamps together, ensuring it is tight.

'This is the hard part,' he mutters, dipping a finger into a pot of grease and smearing it along the seal. He takes up a stopwatch from the mess on the table, clicking it on.

Tick-tick-tick...

The boy moves from foot to foot, the ice on the floor seeping into his flesh. The clock dial whirs.

'I've been working on two minutes...'

Tick-tick-tick...

Uncle Mike bangs the clock to zero and reaches for the pipe. With a cloth he wipes the smear of grease and quickly unhitches the clamps. With a hiss the pipe falls open.

There is the *okker*, the ice already leaving its body. It gasps, one eye still frozen. From behind the dorsal fin a seam of ice runs down its spine.

'*Eat*,' sighs the *okker*, a turning, fading sound in the mind of the boy.

'We need a better way to refrigerate. We need to find a way.'

Uncle Mike pushes a finger into the *okker*'s side. The flesh is ruined, iced sludge.

'What if there was a way? What if we could freeze our catch, and wake them again weeks later? What if we could send the freshest fish all across the world? Then we could compete.'

The boy studies the fish.

'See if you can do anything. Maybe you can dream a way to fix my machine. Maybe you can sing to this fish and make it live, or talk to it, like you do. Maybe it will tell you the secret I am looking for.'

'What about my pearl?' whispers the boy.

'*My* pearl,' says the big man. 'My pearl, to your debt.'

Uncle Mike turns. His shadow retreats. The boy is alone. He studies the pipe, the rig of nozzles, this detritus of Uncle Mike's doing strewn across the workbench.

He places his hand on the ruined fish. Deep down, so quiet that it is a thought behind a thought, he can still the little fish calling.

'*Eat*.'

Gently he places his palm on the ruined head, and gently he crushes it, letting that lonely sound fade.

'It's better so.' He gathers the body and slops it into a bucket. With a cloth he wipes the pipe clean, at the same time testing the rubber seal.

He shakes his head.

'Stupid,' he says, the word forever twisted. 'Shoopid.'

He does not work on the pipe and he does not sing to the dead *okker*. After all, what could he do? Instead he cleans the table and dreams of her.

CHAPTER FOUR

The day begins like all the others – with the dark. This day, though, the dark is split by her. He is smiling as he wakes.

He rolls from his sleeping mat. Laid out on the sandy floor are his trousers and vest and jersey. He puts them on in the dark, and gropes for the matches, striking one and setting shadows to dancing. He sets the black kettle to boil. He nudges the door open with one hand on the handle and the other at the base, pushing against the warping of the seasons so that it bangs out of the old wooden frame. Outside is the flood of the fresh morning, the smell of the new bush, the wash of stars across the sky. The three stars that form the belt of Orion, the hunter, crouch on the horizon, the Southern Cross is long to bed. With no moon, the stars burn.

Is she also watching them?

He walks round to the back of his little hut. Here where there is nothing but veld in the darkness and the mountains beyond, and the boughs of the apple tree spread above him. He reaches up and takes one. The apple is small, and will be sharp and a little bitter, but its sweetness will be there also. The bitter sweetness of the veld. He pockets it with a smile.

His black coffee steams as he drinks it, the heat spreading through his belly. He takes up his *mandjie* – his basket – packed with hook, line, a roll of sinkers and bait, and he strikes off down the starlit track. Sand and grit crunch between his bare toes.

Is she awake? Where did she sleep?

He remembers where they slept, in her cave, past the dark one keeping guard whom she merely touched to sleepiness. '*He's just hungry*,' she'd said, and showed him her sanctuary: the cave painted with clams, each carrying a pearl, the flume that led to the surface and a glimpse of the heavens, that chimney that so many times he had seen ignite with spray on wild days.

He remembers the warmth of being there with her, the wonder of that flame within her breath heating him from the inside. And her touch, her skin. Smooth and sleek and wound around him, her cheek, her ear, her hot mouth. Her eyes.

'God!' he shouts, raising his arms in happiness as he turns down to the beach and his little boat waiting. 'Her mouth!' The world of her mouth, that melting eternity. And her green eyes, touched by the moon's light, at the same time outside him and inside him. '*More*,' she had said as he looked into her and she into him, '*more*.'

'More,' he mutters through his jagged lip as he lends his weight to the boat, now piled with his nets, lifting it from the sand's suck, shucking it one, two, into the shallows. He feels its wooden weight soften as the living water streams in beneath. '*I am flying*,' he thinks.

Today he has petrol, supplied by Uncle Mike for the theft of the pearl. He leaks the sharp smelling fuel into the little motor, unclasps the hinge and lets the propeller sink into the cold sea. He is drifting free, no waves in the bay this morning as he primes, and takes hold, and jerks the starter cable in a high arc – one, two, *bhurrrroooooaaaarrrrr!* The little motor clatters, and the propeller spins, and he turns it to the east where there is still no sun. He glides out of the bay on water so clear that the stars are both in the heavens and the ocean below. Orion wheels on the water, hunting his ever-running prey. This morning there is no horizon, water and sky are one.

But by eleven morning is a distant memory, as is happiness. The sun is high and the day is hot. He has caught nothing. He has laid his nets in three sweeps already. The ocean is not speaking to him. There is no grace today, and there is no her.

He has anchored in the northern channel twice, probing for *harder* with unweighted bait on the surface, letting the current carry his traps in shallow lines, and deeper with lead twisted above the hook, searching for heavier and slower prey, and still nothing. The day is clear but the water is not – red today, the colour that heralds hot and heavy wind coming. He cannot see the fishes below and their talk is scattered, broken apart ahead of the coming weather.

He looks out towards the finger of the Sentinel. Is she there? Although the fish are not hungry, he is. He would dive, but he cannot see. He would not face that dark one without her. He looks up to the sun, burning not far from noon, and he scowls.

Automatically he casts a line, trawling near the surface with sun-warm bait even though he knows nothing will bite.

Yeeeerrrk.

He is up in an instant, whipping the line with an instinctive strike, angling for the jaw side, willing the hook to sink into flesh, but no, the line floats free.

'Dammit,' he mutters into his sparse beard, once again sitting on the gunwale, his green oilskin squeaking against the chipped wood and pulling across the tops of his boots.

'What kind of fish?'

It felt like a big *harder*, but struck like a bottom swimming fish. In frustration he shakes his head, muttering into his T-shirt, his eyes watching the Sentinel and willing her to appear as he pulls the line in, hand over hand.

Yerk!

He's up, striking left this time, working the fish with all his guile.

Tzzzziiinnng!

It's on! The line strafing through the water, cutting down on his *vingerlappie* – his finger rubber – both hands up and plucking the lasering wire to control the fighting fish.

Red water fish! Big fish!

He sits back, his boots wedged against the little boat's walls, and as his right hand frees he reaches down to grab a tail of sacking, not breaking his rhythm, the line biting into him.

'Hold it,' he mutters, realising the fish is above the ten-kilo thread.

He relaxes the pull, giving the creature some leeway, and immediately the thread is plucked from his hands and with it his spool jumps after it, catching and kicking up near the gunwale. He heaves for it, trying to catch the little block of wood, but no, it bounces and spins for a moment above the water, and then it's gone, into the red and under. He watches it go, trailing bubbles.

He shouts in anger, raging in the little boat, beating his cutting board with his bleeding hand.

He knows where the anger lies. His stupidity, he hadn't secured the line, he was fishing for nothing, hoping for something.

'*Dom!* He curses. 'Shoopid fish!'

He puts his hands to his face, everything hot and red behind his closed lids.

'*Where is she?*'

And in the red rage suddenly a new sound: laughter.

He turns, his hands off his eyes, and there she is, her face out of the water, her open mouth laughing and her green eyes laughing into his, and his line in her hand.

'*You!*'

'*You!*'

He rushes to her side of the little boat, leaning over and reaching for her joyfully, but then he is shy and he sits back.

She tilts her head to one side, curious at his behaviour. She swims toward him, coming to rest in the shadow of the little boat, looking up at him.

'*Are you okay?*'

'*Where have you been?*'

'*I was...*' She pauses. '*Is there something wrong?*'

'*I thought you would be here, when I got here this morning. I've been waiting. I didn't think you were coming.*'

'*I was out in the ocean.*'

'*Oh.*'

She holds his line up to him.

'*Nothing biting?*'

'*No.*'

'*It's the wind. It disturbs them.*'

He nods. And then he smiles.

'*I brought you something.*'

He reaches into his tuck box and takes out a wrapped napkin. He holds it out to her.

'*What is it?*'

'*Open it.*'

She takes it, unfolding it as a swell runs beneath them. Kelp rises and so does she and for a moment she is nearly eye level with him. He will not forget that, the way she rose up, her eyes on the gift in her hands.

'*It's an apple. It grew in my garden.*'

She rolls it in her palms.

'*It's so... smooth.*'

'*It's a fruit. Taste it.*'

'*Taste it?*'

'*It's food.*'

She thinks for a moment.

'*I want to do it with you. I want you here.*'

He looks around, scanning the Island for other boats, but they are alone.

'*Would you like to come into the boat?*'

She shakes her head. '*The sun is too hot.*' She sinks further into the cold water, letting it cover her from the burning ball up there. She looks about her. '*What about over there,*' she says, pointing to Seal Rock. '*On the edge there. Can you go there?*'

The rock ends on a shelf covered by the tide. There is a shallow pool, an edge on which to sit with the deep of the channel falling away beside it.

'*I can do that.*'

She is about to dive, the apple held high. A thought crosses her.

'*Please hold this.*'

She holds the green apple out to him, the salt and the ocean's murmur and the clicking of the deep-down *kray* all around them. With both hands she places the apple in his. With both hands he reaches further and puts his hands around her, his body shaking, his heart bursting, and pulls her to him. Her hair all about him, wet with the sea, her cheek next to his, her lips on his, the world upside down.

'*Come,*' she whispers, her mouth hot at his ear. She breaks from him, diving into the red water. He turns to take hold of his motor. There she is, surfacing near the rock, looking back to him.

Bbbraap! as his motor comes to life.

Moments later his little boat is anchored to the flat top of Seal Rock and he is ready to join her. He stands on the rock while she waits in the surging tide.

'*Wait,*' he says, suddenly sitting down to remove his boots.

She watches him, smiling as one foot and then the other is revealed. She reaches out to touch one.

'*Wait!*'

He dips his feet in the water, shaking them to clean them.

She takes one in each hand. He sits forward to the edge of the swirling tidal pool so that she can take his ankles too. She kneads them, feeling the ankle joint and the extension of bones into the foot, taking each toe in her fingers. She looks up to him and giggles.

He lowers himself into the cold water, a shock as it comes flooding in over the top half of his oilskin.

'*Hah!*' he gasps at the cold.

She slides onto his lap. Once again the slow fire she brings begins to burn the water. The cold disappears.

He puts his hands on her stomach and lets them slide down to her hips, where skin turns to tail. He runs his hands down, and down, feeling the whole length of her, his arm arcing out when it reaches the wide spread of her fin. Her body shivers at his touch.

'I was afraid you wouldn't come back. I went swimming, I wanted to forget.'

'I couldn't wait to come back. I looked for you all morning. I thought you were a dream.'

'I'm not a dream.' She shifts herself around to look at him.

'Here.' He reaches into his breast pocket and takes out the apple. He bites it and then holds it out to her, chewing.

She bites. She chews. He is watching her face.

'Do you like it?'

He feels the sensations tumbling in her mouth – the fresh bite of the apple, the sweetness and the bitterness flooding her tongue.

'I like it. I've seen it before, but I've not tasted it.' She takes another bite. *'Sometimes those like you throw them away,'* she says around her mouthful.

'I want to show you other things.'

'Yes?'

'I want to show you all the things on the land, all my things.'

She stops chewing and instead looks him steadily in the eye. *'You will have to bring them to me.'*

He holds her gaze for a moment, and then looks off, to the moving ocean.

'Where are your people? Is that where you were today, with your kind, out in the ocean?'

She shakes her head.

'I am alone.'

He nods, still not looking at her. He is aware of the distance of difference between them.

'Why are you always alone? The others are always in twos.'

'I work better by myself. The others have different ways.'

'They don't hear like you do.'

'No.'

'Why can only you hear us?'

'I don't know.'

'I've spoken to you before, but you didn't know it.'

'I did know it,' he says, suddenly smiling wide. *'I have heard you laughing. I did not know what it was, but now I know. I cannot explain the sea.'*

She puts her hand to his cheek. The water on it is cold, her flesh is hot.

'Fish don't laugh,' she says, kissing him.

'No, they don't. They say only one thing.'

She turns to look at him. *'Eaaatt,'* she says, her beautiful eyes laughing into his.

'Eaaatt,' he replies, laughing with her.

They fall into each other, arms around each other, bodies against each other, laughter clothing them.

The heat rises between them.

He pulls his shirt off and presses his bare chest against her, holding her. She puts her arms over his and squeezes also, closing her eyes. Both sense the coming pain, but feel it only as desire.

'There is something I want to show you. Something I'm sure you have never seen.'

'What is it?'

'I'm going to show you. A sight you cannot see from the water. A sight of the land.'

She squeezes him.

'I can't leave the water. I will dry out.'

'I will make a way. You will see. I will show you something beautiful that you have never seen, and you will not be harmed. I promise you.'

'For you, I will try.'

The tide washes over them.

Finally he must leave. Back in his boat, he looks down at her.

'Will you be here tomorrow?'

'I will be here every day that you look for me.'

His chest burns.

'Early?'

'Yes.'

'Sunup?'

'*Yes!*'

His heart sings.

He is about to go, his propellor lowered into the water.

'*Wait!*' she calls suddenly.

She dives, and is gone.

The sea washes foam on the surface, the water the red of the coming wind. In the distance the land crouches in a smear of brown, radiating heat. He floats, drifting now, his anchor stowed in the hatch.

And then he hears it, a thousand of them.

'*Eeeeaaatt!*'

He jumps up, he can feel them coming, an up-rushing of a thousand souls.

'*Eeeaaaatt!*'

Like torpedoes they rise up out of the red water, like a silver cloud they hang in the noontime air, flapping and bending and full of sun-refracted spray, and then they come slapping down all over the boat, all over him, filling the world with their twisting bodies.

'*Eat!*' they moan as they land in drifts and piles.

And through it all he sees her circling under the surface, her teeth bared, a wolf that herds them. And he hears her.

'*Eat!*' she whispers in their tongue, as they fly, and die.

Soon his boat is full. He wallows home as the red wind finally comes, rising in a line on the water that rushes across the soupy red, turning it all white. A following wind, speeding his passage.

The afternoon is slow at the factory. The ladies have finished their sorting and stand in their own drifts and piles, cigarettes out, waiting for *chaila* – quitting time. High above two hawks wheel, searching the brown hills with sharp eyes.

On the dark road snaking through the land a boy is pulling a cart. It trundles and groans, bursting with fish.

The women stop their smoking when he appears. It is a huge catch, anyone can tell – a catch of the old days.

'Uncle!'

Uncle Mike comes sauntering through the throng.

'What's this now?' and he stops also when he sees the cant of the cart, and the grin on the boy's face. There they lie, a thousand of them, filling the cart to overflow.

'It was a good day,' says the boy, casually unhitching himself from his yoke, 'I knew it would be, because of the wind.'

'How did...'

'Luck always has to change. It was time.' There is an air about the boy as he sets the yoke down before the scale, a confidence. Salie is there with wide eyes, his notebook and pencil at the ready.

'This is a full quota,' says the boy to Salie. 'I'm looking for full price.'

Salie can do nothing but nod as he runs his eye over the catch.

'You'll get your price,' says Uncle Mike. He steps forward to spread a hand between the boy's shoulders, steering him gently from the sorting line. The boy looks back as Salie begins to slop fish to the scale, taking the chance to look the women in the eye also. *His* catch. But Uncle Mike is walking him out of the sorting house and into the bright sun. Above them the hawks wheel.

'How did you do it?'

The boy turns to the man towering over him. He smiles. 'I was just lucky.'

Uncle Mike smiles also. 'There is an important meeting today. It might be a good idea for you to come. In one hour, at Van Deventer's place. Come. Let's go and look at the books and get you paid. You will make up for the last month with today's catch!'

He steers the boy towards the office doors to the left of the loading bay. The boy's smile is gone. *A meeting?* His eyes find the ground. He does not listen as Uncle Mike talks to him of wind and tide and reef. Weeds grow in the cracks in the concrete, today tipped with yellow flowers.

CHAPTER FIVE

Van Deventer's place is another processing factory a little bigger than Uncle Mike's. It is a place the boy has passed many times, peering in past the large white gate looking out onto the main road, but he has never been inside. The seven *fabriek* owners of the Baai are all here: Van Deventer, Mostert, Weatherall-Thomas, the Schaafsma brothers – Nico and Mark, Uncle Mike, and old Thys Mocke, who has been in the Baai longer than anyone. They have come in their shiny pickup trucks and they are worried men. They are clustered together around Van Deventer's truck in the forecourt, discussing the sea.

Uncle Mike and the boy stay seated in Uncle Mike's little motor, from there they study the gathering of the town's fisher kings. The grouped men wear boots like Uncle Mike's, felt-lined and snug, and strong jeans that cover stocky legs, and pocketed shirts and brimmed hats, and all of them have gold bands circled around their ring fingers. Their fingers are thick, their arms, their hands know work. These are predatory men, but today they are prey.

'You know them?'

'I know Mr Mocke,' murmurs the boy, remembering the day the old man came to the *fabriek*. He had greeted the boy and held out his hand to him.

His eyes were blue and sparkled with kindness. The boy had liked him then, and likes him still.

The boy is nervous. He is unaccustomed to the clothing Uncle Mike has given him – a pair of shining white running shoes, and jeans bitten in at the waist with a newly punched belt too big for his lean hips. And a clean shirt. When last did he wear a clean shirt? A shirt without holes?

'What must I do?'

'You caught a full load today. Out of everyone that went to sea, in the whole Baai today the catch was five. Not even the foreigners caught today.' He points to the men. 'They asked for you to come.'

'They asked for me?'

'They want to know how you did it.'

'But I told Uncle. I just got lucky.'

Uncle Mike snorts. 'Lucky? You? You are not lucky.'

Uncle Mike brings a packet of mints out of his denim pocket. He tears it open at the top and offers one to the boy. 'Just tell them how you did it. Where you caught, what line, just tell them. We will see what we can get out of it.'

He pops the mint into his mouth.

'Come, let's go stand with them.'

The mint is sharp, dissolving on his tongue with a sting he does not like. His anxiety is sharp also.

'Come,' repeats Uncle Mike as he climbs up out of the little car and strides over to them.

The boy swallows.

He clicks the door open and steps out into the hot sun. The men regard him from under their brimmed hats and behind their loud smiles. They watch as he tentatively closes the door and sidles over to them. The boy hears them snicker – *who is this little fool to be meeting with men?*

Abruptly, the boy halts his stride. He crouches to tie a shoelace that does not need tying, full of the instinct with which he can hook any fish. He has stopped to listen. He can hear their sniggering, see their posturing, even their anger, but there is something more.

'*Eat*,' they all sigh, under the laughing, right at the core of them. '*Eat*,' they whisper in fear.

'*Eat*.'

The boy smiles, his long shadow his companion on the sun-swept concrete. He realises that he knows them. They are animals, just like every other creature. He knows how to catch those that are hungry.

'We just don't have the capital to compete with them,' says Van Deventer. 'They are first world.'

The men are seated in Van Deventer's boardroom. They are spread around a hexagonal cluster of triangular tables, a cloth over it all, each perched on a white plastic chair. The room is too small for them. The walls crowd them in, the table is too big. Windows cover two sides; beyond them the sorting hall lies idle. In the old days, in the season, it would run night and day with rotating crews.

'Mikey? What progress with your fridge?'

Uncle Mike shrugs like they do, meaty shoulders raised and iron fingers threading through each other.

'It's all guesswork. I'm making progress, but for a reliable system we are looking at years, not months.'

The men shrug and grind their fingers and look worried together.

'The fish stocks are not what they used to be,' says fat Mr Mostert, stroking his moustache. 'In the years gone by...'

'The fish are out there,' blusters Weatherall-Thomas, jabbing a finger to the table. 'We can see them on the monitors. Less fish, yes, but fish! Why are they not biting?'

The eyes of the six shift to Uncle Mike. He looks over his shoulder to where the boy stands at the door.

'Jonny-boy. Where did you make your catch today? Tell us what happened.'

The boy clears his throat. He has been waiting for them to call on him, and the hooks of fear have been waiting also. Now the fear comes banging in his belly and up through his chest. It closes his throat and puts sweat on his brow. '*They are hungry*,' he tells himself desperately, '*they are hungry and all they want is to eat.*'

'I was at the *gat* today – the well at the Island,' he whispers into his sparse beard. 'I laid nets all morning but got no *kray*, no nothing, even though I could hear them.'

'What's he saying?' barks Van Deventer. 'Mikey, what's he saying?'

'Give him a chance,' says Uncle Mike. 'Jonny, speak up boy. Come closer.'

The boy nods and takes a small step towards them.

'I threw lines in the north channel,' he whispers, no more loudly than before. 'At the Island, even out by the *diep* reef – the deep reef. Nothing.'

'Can't hear him,' says Nico.

'Speak up, Jonny,' says Uncle Mike.

The boy takes a deep breath. He opens his mouth wide, but the sound does not come.

'He doesn't speak good,' growls Uncle Mike. 'He says he was at the *gat* by the Island, he caught nothing. He threw lines in the north channel and even out by the *diep* reef. Nothing.'

'What did your monitor say? Was there fish?' asks fat Mostert.

'I have no monitor,' whispers the boy.

'Did he say no monitor?'

'He doesn't fish with a monitor,' says Uncle Mike.

'I know the Island, and I know the fish,' continues the boy, his eyes closed and his fists at his sides. 'They were there but not biting. It was because of the wind. They were waiting for the wind to turn.'

'Did he say wind?' asks Mocke.

'Red water, yes. Berg wind. Carry on boy.'

'I had to wait for it to turn. The fish don't like it building up, they want it to blow. I waited for them, and just before the wind came...'

The seven lean in, food on their minds.

'...then they started.'

The boy pauses, remembering the thousand bodies glittering in the sun.

'I caught the whole boat in forty-five minutes. I was catching them just arm deep, one breath after dropping the line.'

'But everyone had their lines out when the wind turned. Why did you catch so well?' Van Deventer asks from his place at the head of the table.

'He knows fish,' says Uncle Mike, cutting off the boy's reply. 'He is my best fisherman. No one at my place can out-catch him, and I would bet no one in the Baai either.'

The boy shrugs. His slim shoulders reach up to meet his ears, his fingers folding together like wings.

'I was just lucky.'

'Lucky,' snorts Mostert. 'That's not lucky. That's a miracle.'

The talk drifts away from the boy and on to the foreigners' ships. The boy sits back and listens.

'*Eat*,' he hears.

The meeting ends with the seven having decided nothing, but having left their fears in a pile together on the table, burned up in three great ashtrays. Once again the boy steps into the little motor with Uncle Mike, and once again they take the snaking road home.

'What will they do?'

'It's a tough thing to get everyone to decide.'

Around them dusk has settled. Lights shine in the few homes scattered around the central convenience store. Bright rooms, inside them fishermen and fisherwomen tending to their children, attending to supper. The day was long and hot, and now the night is here to cool them.

Uncle Mike clicks his indicator and to its ticking he pulls into the convenience store parking lot, alongside the open sweep of the petrol station.

'You did well today.'

He removes a palm of money from his breast pocket, holding it out to the boy. 'You are still far behind on your quota, but you deserve this. A bonus for your catch today, and for coming with me. You did well. You talked well.'

The boy takes it.

'Fish well tomorrow. I'm looking forward to another big catch.'

By the neon light of the petrol station the boy looks to the hills. The settling night is warm. The crest of the hills is far above, a line of dark against the purple sky. With a smile he places the notes in his pocket.

Money.

He has not had money before.

And now he has a plan.

The following day, once the catching is done, the boy hands that same money to Mr Hofmeyr of the hardware shop. Together, they select a pile of lumber.

The boy carts the wood home. Instead of the distant hills to his left and the glittering ocean to his right, he sees the whorls and knots of wood in his mind's eye.

Once back at his hut he unloads the lumber onto his patch of sand. Having brewed a cup of coffee he seats himself at the rough table, and allows the lumber to speak. Slowly, joint for joint and nail for nail, the shape of it forms in his mind. Finally, it is done, and all he must do is build it.

He sets to.

Days pass in the little village of the Baai, as the sun replaces the moon, and the winds wash the land clean. One morning, as dawn is breaking, he waits for her at the landing zone. Beside him he has the product of a week's labour. Standing resplendent on varnished wheels is a beautiful cart, fashioned on the design of his old one. There is a load bed ready to transport fish, and a yoke for him to pull it, but thereafter it is so much more. Every panel is carved, the sea's creatures swimming through the wood. The load bed is meticulously sealed so that it is watertight, and built into the centre is a second chamber, double sealed, in which a second load of water can be held, hidden from the sun. On the sides of the cart are pegs and clips holding all he might need for a two-day journey. Water-skins, rope, rifle, pan. It is a cart that is the best of him, made for her.

He has chosen a Saturday when he knows they will be alone. The water is still and low, kelp floating in thick islands in the shallows and glistening in slowly moving clumps. Across the horizon the dawn is coming, pink.

He feels her before he sees her. She is in the bay, making her careful way to him. She slides between the kelp, a graceful hand parting their long stalks as she moves through, aware of him also.

She is nervous.

He is nervous.

'*Don't be nervous*,' she whispers from out there, down there.

'*Don't be nervous*,' he replies, and smiles.

He holds the yoke of his new cart in his hand. Absently he kneads the smooth-sanded wood. 'How will it be?' he wonders. 'Will she want to come?'

She breaks the surface, water streaming off her. Her eyes are nervous, but they are eyes just for him.

They cannot touch, not yet.

He has placed a brick as a brake against the new cart's wheel, and now he tips it away with his toe. Released, the new cart bounces down the little slipway. Cold water swirls through its open rear door, filling the load bed. From the shore he pushes so that it submerges fully.

'*Will you get in?*'

Tentatively she glides into the enclosed cube of new wood. Still, they have not touched.

'*I'm going to close the door.*'

She bites her lip as he wades in to chest height. He is now near her, near enough to touch. Reaching out he releases a bolt, first on one side and then on the other. He works the door into place, making sure that it is sealed.

Now they are only inches apart.

She reaches out to him, her fingers through his hair. Her mouth on his. Her mouth is the ocean. She is the ocean.

The world explodes with the coming sunrise.

Her eyes shine with love.

His eyes shine with love.

'*Morning*,' she breathes.

His wet face breaks into a shaggy-dog smile.

'*Morning*.'

He puts his cheek against hers. How warm it is.

'*How are you going to pull me out?*'

He holds a finger in front of his smiling face.

'*Watch and see.*'

She giggles.

He swims excitedly around the new cart until he finds his footing and then sloshes up the slipway.

'*I thought of everything.*'

He attacks his waiting winch that is looped by chain to a tree, a frayed orange-and-white rope trailing down to the new cart where it is tied by bowline to a tow hitch. The rope rises up, taught, as he whirls the handle, and slowly the cart begins to move.

She holds onto the lip, peering over the edge as the water falls away, and suddenly she is above the land. Her knuckles whiten on the wood. For the first time, she is out of the water. The cart jolts on the uneven slipway. She has never felt that before, the jolt of gravity and air, the kick of it.

'*What if it leaks?*'

He shakes his head and looks up to her green eyes. '*I promise you.*'

'*How will you pull it?*'

She swirls from side to side in her sealed cube. For the first time, the ocean is over there.

'*I'm strong. I have been pulling my cart all my life.*'

He threads the rope out of the winch, winding it in a loop and hanging it from a peg on the cart's side. Then he takes up the yoke and puts it across his chest. He leans forward. The weight builds in his legs, through his back, and finally merges in the centre of the yoke. The cart begins to move as his bare toes pull through the sand.

She turns to see the ocean receding while the sun frees herself from the lightening bay.

'*Where are we going?*'

'*It's my turn to take you somewhere you have never been,*' he says.

CHAPTER SIX

What she notices most is the breeze. Every plant shivers as it passes. She knows only the current, the slow to and fro of deep to shallow, but here the current is in the air and it sets the fields dancing.

'*It's flower season*,' he says, pointing to a field dusted with the pink, yellow and white of thousands of freshly opened blossoms. '*They come every year, just after the rain*.'

He picks one and passes it to her.

'*Do you know the rain?*'

She holds the flower to her nose. Underwater scent is different, like the current it is heavier, it drips through the senses, winding its way through water. But up here the flower's scent tumbles into her, filling her with its pollen. She crushes the stem between her fingers. There too, the scent of moisture, sap, and a green stain across her fingertips. She puts her finger to her tongue. Sweet.

'*Can you eat it?*'

He picks another flower and bites off its head.

His smile spreads across his face, a child's grin. She will remember that, looking down at him from her perch. She eats the flower too. It crunches between her teeth, all the colour of the flower-dusted field disintegrating in her mouth. She smiles back at him.

They trundle on.

Hills that were at first far away draw near.

'*There are no people here?*'

'*No, I'm the only one that comes here.*'

Soon the hills rear up around them. They pass into their shadow. It grows cool.

'*Where are we going?*'

'*You showed me the deep of the ocean, something I have never seen,*' he says, his voice short against the pull of the yoke. '*I want to do the same.*'

The ground begins to rise as they enter the foothills. He plods on, his gait steady, the cart creaking.

White and yellow sandstone rears beside them. She reaches out to brush her fingertips against it. It crumbles, leaving a smear of rock in her palm. She brushes her hands together, marvelling at the crushed rock washing against her skin. It is dry.

'*What is your name?*' he asks.

She sees only his back, bunched up against the yoke, his calves tightening and releasing as his feet pull them higher.

'*What is a name?*'

'*What do they call you?*'

'*Who?*'

'*There is no one that talks with you?*'

'*My guardian talks with me.*'

'*What does he call you?*'

'*Little one.*'

The cart creaks.

'*Then that is your name.*'

The air is hot around her, heat she has never felt. It radiates off the stones. She sinks deeper into her wooden tank, letting the water cover all but her head. The only sound is the creak of the cart's wheels.

'*What is yours?*'

'*Jonothan.*'

'*Who gave it to you?*'

'*I don't know. I have always been called Jonothan.*'

Suddenly he pauses and slips the yoke from his body. He turns and soundlessly lifts his rifle from its rack at the front of the cart. With his eyes he motions for her to look.

Above them, near the crest of the cliff rising above them, stands an animal. Four-legged and covered in fur it looks out beyond them, down the track to the open fields below.

The boy raises his rifle, holding his aim and steadying his breathing. A crack, the kick of the bullet against rock and the animal falls, tumbling down to them.

It lodges above them, kicking. The boy swarms up to meet it, a blade in his hand. It is not necessary.

'*What is it?*'

'*This is a rock rabbit. We will eat it tonight.*' He smiles at her. '*When I show you the second thing you have never seen.*'

The animal is tied to the cart. The boy hauls them upwards.

The road beneath them begins to level, and the walls beside them sink. His gait eases as he leads them out onto a plateau. Ahead of them is an ocean of grass, sweeping down and away. Far below they can see the rash of the settlement, the clusters of houses and the larger factories gathered on the coast. The harbour with its breakwater is a distant line in the glittering blue, and beyond that the vast ocean, from horizon to horizon.

'*I thought you have probably never been high up before.*'

She is up straight in her tank, looking out at all of it.

'*There is the factory where I take my catch,*' he tells her, pointing to the east. His finger travels left across the long coast. '*And there is my home...*' And his finger travels further still, '*... and there is yours. The Island.*'

She looks out upon all of it, this vast new world. And then a thought takes her and she turns. Behind them, stretching away in a sea as endless as the blue, the hills undulate seemingly forever. A road out there, white gravel winding through the hills. In the distance a dust cloud where a motor travels. To the south another road, the tar tributary of the main drag that runs along the coast, connecting the factories to each other, and to the world.

'*What are those?*'

'*The roads?*'

'*Yes. The roads.*'

'*They are channels on which people travel.*'

Both look out on the wide expanse.

'*There is a whole world out there. There are cities out there, places where people live, schools of people, shoals of them.*'

'*Have you been there?*'

'*No, I have never.*'

And she looks out to the west, where the sun is making its slow descent. There mountains brood, impassive and dark against the lowering orb behind them.

'*And what is out there?*'

'*There is nothing out there. Just mountains, forever.*'

Flames dance blue and orange between the dried brush he has collected, eating the wood. She watches the dancing. Above them the stars roar.

She holds her hand out to the fire, the heat building in her flesh until the pain glows white and she jerks it away and douses her palm in the water.

He cleans the rock rabbit he has killed, then skewers it and places it above the flames. The flesh begins to blacken.

'*Why could we not stay on the hilltop?*' Her eyes stay fixed on the flames. '*I wanted to look at the lights of the houses.*'

'*I didn't want anyone to see our fire. If we can see them, they can see us. I don't want anyone to know that we are up here.*'

They have retreated to a hollow in the sandstone where the walls sweep up overhead, the orange of the flames flickering against the rock. The first drop of rabbit fat falls, sizzling on the coals.

'*Have you ever seen fire?*'

'*I saw a boat with fire once. Two men were out at sea. Their sail was burning.*'

'*I wanted this to be the first time you saw it.*'

'*I have never seen it like this.*'

She runs her hands along the lip of her tank, the smooth sanded wood soft against her palms, every joint perfect, every carved creature her own.

'*Look at this.*' He leans forward and blows into the flames. They burn brighter. The rabbit blackens.

'*Do it again!*'

He takes a burning log and holds it up to her. The flame dances before her eyes. Gently she purses her lips together, and gently she blows. The flame jumps up brighter, flickering in the dark. She blows harder, sending it higher, and then it is snuffed out.

'*Oh.*'

He blows gently, goading the embers that pulsate along the wood. They glow orange, brightening, until with a puff a flame dances again.

'*Gently,*' she says.

'*Yes. Gently.*'

He slices the blackened flesh of the rabbit. The meat is pink inside and steaming. She accepts the slice of meat and places it on her tongue. The juice seeps into her, the memory of its blood reduced to salt. She chews slowly, rolling the seared meat around in her mouth, until her face sours and she spits it onto the ground.

'*I'm sorry!*'

He laughs, flicking the meat into the fire. '*Why don't you like it?*'

'*It's too strange. It's too hot. I like fish.*'

'*I like fish too.*'

'*Do you mind?*'

'*You can't like it all,*' he says, standing and coming to her, putting his cheek to hers.

'*Come in here with me.*'

He chews his meat, thinking. '*Wait.*' He reaches for his bucket. '*I don't want anything bad to happen.*'

He dips the bucket into her tank, filling it so that the level in the cart lowers a little, and places it on the ground. He places his foot on the wheel, steadying himself.

'*You can't get in with your clothes on.*'

He pauses.

'*You have to take them off.*' She whispers this to him, her green eyes dancing with fun.

'*I'll get cold!*'

'*No, you won't.*'

Shyly, he pulls his shirt over his head and drops it to the ground. Shyly, he unbuttons his tattered trousers and leg by leg steps out of them. The marks of every day he has toiled on this earth are there for her to see.

'*Come.*' She reaches out to him.

He slips in behind her and folds her in his arms. Together, they look up to the stars. All the world is in her, and him.

'*Look,*' she hears him saying, feeling the ripple of his voice in the water. '*That is Orion. The three stars of Orion. Do you know them?*' His words unfold within her like a growing sunrise.

'*I know them. I see them up there, at night, when the days are hot.*'

'*Yes. They are summer stars.*'

'*Summer?*'

'*The days of heat.*' He squeezes his arms about her, crushing her to fullness, filling her.

'*That is summer?*'

'*These days are what we call summer.*'

She presses his hands with her own, resting her head into the living beauty of his shoulder.

'*We have a story about them. Do you want to know it?*'

She nods, and he feels the movement of her head as a miracle too, a rustle on his skin that will come to him when one day his life peels from this world.

'*Those three bright ones are the belt of a hunter. See if you can see him...*' He traces the line of a shoulder from a waist, and two legs, and a weapon held in the hunter's celestial hand. '*It is a bow he hunts with. Do you know a bow? It is like the spears fishermen throw at the seals, a machine to throw the spear from their hand.*'

'*There, that bright star, do you see it?*' He points to Sirius a million leagues away. '*That is his hunting dog, it follows him as he hunts the animals of the world. The story says that he travelled the world, hunting and killing, and no animal could escape his bow. They say he could speak with the animals; he could hear their thoughts...*'

She laughs a little, and he laughs too.

'*...so that he always knew where they would be, and how they would try to escape him. He became so great that he boasted that he would kill every creature on this earth to prove it.*' He pauses, the silence of the stars echoing back.

'*And so?*' she asks.

'*Gaia, the god of the earth...*'

'*God?*'

'*God...*' He pauses for a moment, the world seeming to listen as he searches for the truth. '*God ... the source of life.*'

She nods then, understanding him well. She knows God. It is the movements of the tiniest *treurvissie* – the sorrow fish – as it flicks before her in the waters. It is the sweep of a *rhone* whale as it rises from the blue and towers over her, and it is her alone, listening to the endless quiet of the open ocean, a hundred miles from shore.

'*I know God.*'

The boy holds her tighter. He knows God also. God is the one that moves her fingers and makes her thoughts appear within him when she speaks, as clear as a flower in the field. God is her breathing body, her heat.

'*You are God,*' she whispers, but he does not hear her. '*Tell me the story.*'

'*Well, Gaia heard Orion's boasting, and she was angry because all the creatures are her own. So, she sent the most dangerous creature to kill him.*'

'*What was it?*'

The boy raises his arm to the sky. '*It is a scorpion,*' he says, searching among the stars. '*It cannot be seen now. They are winter stars.*' His finger drops down to the southern horizon. '*Do you know a scorpion?*'

'*No.*'

'*Wait.*' He gets up, and she is filled with loss at his going.

'*I won't be long*,' he says, as he disappears into the dark.

'*Come back!*'

'*I won't be long!*'

'*Jonothan!*'

He appears again, his hand held up, and from his fingers a creature is curling in the flickering light.

'*A scorpion.*'

She reaches for the twisting thing.

'*Be careful. Its tail is poison.*'

And she sees the bulb that he holds between his finger and thumb. She understands. This little creature is the assassin sent to defend the honour of Gaia's beautiful world.

'*I understand. This little creature is a brave one.*'

'*It is*,' agrees the boy, before stooping to let the creature disappear into the rocks. Carefully he returns to the water, and she to the circle of his arms, and he to the wild pleasure of her.

'*And so that is the scorpion*,' he murmurs, his voice pulled low. '*It chases the hunter across the sky, defending the wishes of the Goddess.*'

'*And Orion continues his hunting*,' she murmurs, turning to face him, and putting her mouth on his. '*He tries to sting the hunter, forever.*'

The beautiful night draws on.

The stars shift in the heavens.

Waking and sleep merge, he cannot tell what is her body and what is his own, what is a dream and what is not. All is their warmth.

Towards dawn, whether it is a dream or real there begins a singing, a sound of the ocean causing the water to vibrate as the song reaches up, filling the near-vanished night.

He knows he has heard this song before, whether asleep or waking. He has always heard it, he realises, a song he has known all his life.

'*Eat*,' she moans, her cry filling the heavens.

He cannot be sure whether it is during sleep or waking, but just before dawn, when the stars have already begun to wane, he drops his head back and sings with her.

'*Eat,*' he sings, joining her desire.

Her song is of the deep, a sonar click from the heart of creation. Her song is his own.

It is early the next morning that they make their way back. They are not the same. Where they were two that went away to see the veld, the bush, and the mountains, they are one that is returning. He still walks ahead of her pulling the yoke, and she still marvels at the dance of muscle beneath his skin, and always she watches his calves, and ankles, and feet, those endless fascinations, but now they are not a stranger's calves, ankles, and feet, they are his, and more mysterious than ever. In his movements is the new truth that moves in her. They are one. This is the greatest mystery.

'*I want to stop at my home.*' He says it without turning to look at her, absorbed in the complexity of men and the world to which they are returning. With him she is safe, but with them?

'*I left some water there for you.*' He turns to face her as he says it. His heart squeezes as he catches those green eyes. He looks away, back to the path, and then again, a look back at her. Now she leans on the lip of her tank, her head low, her lips apart.

'*What are you looking at?*'

He laughs and breathes in deeply, the oxygen flooding his heart so that it expands even wider, reaching back to her, and ahead, to their future together.

'*We won't be long. I must get you back to the ocean.*' He mutters this, he does not want her to hear.

'*Is that your home?*' She is pointing ahead to the lone hut on the edge of the veld with its patchwork of timber, its zinc roof, and the fence that runs around it. '*This is where you live?*'

'*It is,*' he affirms as he brings the cart up to his water tanks, pulling it in alongside them. There is a new tank there, a third. He knocks the lid from it and takes up the bucket on the cart's side.

He begins to scoop the water in and around her. But she is not looking. Instead, she is peering through the window set flush in its wooden frame.

Inside is the mattress against a wall, the low table next to it, the shelf and the gas cooker, and the kettle. She knows none of these things. His things, his mind. All of it strange and wonderful to her.

'*Can we go inside?*'

'*I think we should get back to the sea.*'

'*Just for a little. I want to see your things.*'

He looks up at her. Her smile.

'*You can carry me. It won't take long.*'

He reaches up and she greets him with a kiss. He folds his arms around her, ready to take her weight, when he hears it: the distant buzzing of a motor. The shock in his body is palpable. She clasps her hands into his flesh, she can feel his fear.

'*Wait, wait.*'

He avoids her eyes, pushing her back into the tank, peeling her hands from him but not letting them go. His eyes study the wood of the cart as his brain speeds. '*You must stay here.*' He looks up at her finally, having masked the fear in his eyes.

'*What is it?*'

'*You must stay here.*'

She nods.

He turns and pries the window open. He slides in through the open frame. Once inside he looks back at her.

'*Stay hidden.*'

With that he is gone, padding to the front door and cracking it open with a hand on the handle and a foot at the base, knocking it open.

Her heart hammers. Beyond him a white machine pulls up, trailing dust. Inside sits the largest man she has ever seen. He stares out from beneath bushy brows, and stiff hair bristles around his mouth. His jaw works, tension writhing beneath his ears. His big knuckles stretch white around the wheel in his hands. He turns to look into the hut and she catches his gaze, fancying he looks straight into her eyes. It freezes her. This is the gaze of a shark, the gaze of death. She sinks down into the water, trembling.

'Where have you been?'

His voice cuts through her. It booms in the cart, in the water, in her heart.

'I was hunting. In the veld.'

She does not understand the words, but she can feel them. A sudden silence is as awful as their voices. She peers up over the lip. Through the window she sees him standing over her love, a head taller and twice as wide.

'Get your oilskin, we need to go to sea.'

He turns back to his little motor.

'I can't come now.'

'Something's happened. Come. We need to go.' He cranks the driver door open, ready to lower his bulk down into the cab.

'I can't come now.'

'Why not? Hurry up. I need you.' He turns the ignition, the engine whirring to life.

'I won't come now. I'll come in an hour.'

'Just get in the car!'

'No.'

A rustle, a murmur of movement out there.

'Salie has cut his hand, he can't steer. We need you. We have to go, now!'

'I can't come now. I'll come in an hour. Wait for me at the harbour.'

'Jonny. Come!'

The silence lengthens. She cannot resist, she must look up. She peers over the ledge to see the man bristling, again standing beside his machine.

'Come now. Get in the motor.'

'I can't come now.'

'What must you do now?'

'I must pray. I can come in a hour.'

'Jonothan!' shouts the big man suddenly. 'Come! Now!' He takes a stride round the little motor, covering the ground at speed. The boy stands rooted.

'I have to pray now. It's Sunday.'

Their voices have changed. There is terrible menace in them. She can feel it, but she does not yet know what it means. Rage fills the big man's eyes.

She cannot look away. He reaches into the machine and pulls out a stick. At the same time her love turns to run, but the big man is as quick as an eel and he smashes that stick into the shoulder of her love, knocking him to the ground. Her love does not make a sound.

The man takes a step toward him and again wields the stick through the sky and grunts as he thuds it into the shoulder of her love, who is lying on the ground, saying nothing.

Another thud.

'I can't come now. I will come in one hour,' he whispers.

The man looks down at the boy's arm. It shudders. And the shoulder. He shakes his big head.

'Bah!' he shouts. 'One hour! I will see you there in one hour.' He strides to the motor, throwing his stick into it, and guns the engine. 'Why must you be so difficult?' There is a clatter of pistons and he is gone.

The boy waits for the motor to disappear down the sandy track, and then he hurries round the side of the hut to her. He is holding his arm tightly to his side.

'*Come, we must go.*'

He is already taking up the yoke.

'*How is your arm?*'

He is already pulling the cart.

'*You should stay down. There could be people around now.*'

She slips down beneath the water and stays quiet as they bump and slosh along the track.

'*Jonothan?*'

He does not answer.

'*My love?*'

He does not reply, but the wheels turn.

She hears him attach the cart to the winch and feels the cart cant over, and slip down the slipway, and feels the cold of her world washing against the side. Clunk, and clunk, as he pulls the pins on either side and lifts the rear door, and her warm water washes out and so does she, back into the ocean. The water's cold fills her suddenly, piercing a route into her heart.

'Let me see your arm.'

'I must go. I will find you later.'

She draws back from him, retreating into the first of the kelp forests filling the bay.

'I'm sorry. I will see you soon.'

'I'm sorry.'

'I will see you soon.'

Her love turns and makes his way back up to the tree. He works the winch, pulling the cart back up onto the sand. There he ties it off, and then jogs down the road, his arm pulled tight to his stomach. He will have to run to the harbour. From the kelp she can see the cart, standing tilted and empty, drying in the sun.

She turns and slips away.

CHAPTER SEVEN

The seven are waiting for him at the quayside. His breath whistles in his throat, his lungs burn, and he holds his arm tightly to his side. All of their expressions are dark. As soon as they see him they turn and step onto a waiting ski-boat. The craft is sleek, fresh-painted red and blue, the name *Sea Queen* curling along its side in white letters. Mr Mostert's best private craft. The boy knows it well. Many days he has seen it anchored at the reef beyond the northern channel.

Uncle Mike lays a hand on the boy's shoulder.

'We want a blue sailfish. Can you do that for us? We want a beautiful fish.'

The boy nods, pulling away from his touch as pain shoots through his forearm and pools in his shoulder. The hand does not let go. Instead it grips his flesh harder.

'We must get one.' Uncle Mike whispers in the boy's ear, his mouth close enough for his breath to touch the skin. 'We must impress our guest.'

Uncle Mike looks over to the ski-boat, prompting the boy to glance over too. Suddenly, the pain ceases. There, standing among the seven is a new man. A man slipped into an oilskin like all of them, a man at ease with the wind and sea like all of them, with crow's feet from staring into the sun like all of them, but unlike them, a man with a shock of hair as dark as tar, combed back, with eyes just as dark behind slanted lids. He is a man such as Jonothan has never seen before, a foreigner from the other side of the world. He looks directly at him.

'We must impress *him.*' Uncle Mike's hand digs into his shoulder once more, a final warning, before he strides to the quayside and steps down, crossing the sea between quay and craft. The boy stands a moment more, intent on the foreigner, his way of blending in but not at all, and then he hurries to release the bow line and send it sailing to the craft, and releases the aft line, and steps over the widening gap as the boat floats free.

The seven eye the boy as he steps onto the ski-boat: his gnarled and bare feet, his tattered trousers, his holed shirt. Mr Van Deventer steps forward, intent on talking to the boy who will pilot his boat. But old Mr Mocke stops him with a hand.

'Stay with our guest, Jaco,' says the old man, gently guiding Van Deventer to the stern of the boat. 'I'll talk to him.'

Mr Mocke joins the boy at the wheelhouse. He puts a friendly hand on Jonothan's own and leans in with friendly eyes.

'You know this boat?'

Jonothan nods, relieved to be confronted by the kind face.

'You can pilot it?'

He nods.

'Uncle Mike says you can get us a blue sailfish?'

'Yes Mr Mocke,' he whispers, believing it with all his heart.

Mr Mocke gestures to the screen of the Foruno Echo Sound, mounted above the wheel. 'We are looking for a big fish. Anything over fifty kilos.'

The boy nods.

Mr Mocke observes this face. It is one that has never seen the inside of a school, the sparse beard does a poor job of hiding the boy's sad upper lip. It is an ignorant face, but undoubtedly a face of the wind and the water, of kicking and blood, a face full of the wisdom of the sea.

'You know how to use the Foruno?'

The boy shrugs. 'Yes, sir. I have been fishing for many years.'

'I know you have. You will do very well.'

Mr Mocke clasps him on the shoulder, an act of encouragement that does not know the pain it causes. 'Do you have a jacket? We are going out deep, it will get cold.'

'*Nee, meneer*. No, sir.'

Mr Mocke slides open a panel beside the wheel. He pulls from it a stained bomber jacket, painted with old fish muck.

'You can wear this.'

'Thank you,' whispers the boy. He holds the jacket to his chest, not wanting to risk revealing his injury by putting it on.

'We'll get you some boots,' Mr Mocke says, eyeing the boy's toes clutching the rough, red-painted deck. Again he clasps the boy's shoulder, and then turns to rejoin the men.

The boy watches. He sees them shuffle awkwardly, avoiding looking at him while shooting glances at Uncle Mike. He knows they do not trust him at all. He flicks his eyes to the foreigner, and with a shock finds those dark eyes watching his own. The foreigner smiles, before slipping a pair of sunglasses onto his face.

The boy turns away quickly. He lets his hands settle on the controls. He closes his eyes. Through the polished chrome of the wheel and the smooth plastic of the throttle he feels every part of the craft beneath his feet. The men with their unfriendly faces fill him with anxiety. They are unknown and frightening. But this craft, even though he has never piloted it, fills him with peace. He knows it like he knows the sea, like he knows fish, like he knows his own breath. Smoothly, he clicks the twin Yamaha 120s into reverse.

The *Sea Queen* pounds across the ocean, her twin motors set to full so that she skips above the swell, the rhythm lulling all onboard. The men of the Baai have naturally found lees of protection against the driving spray, and they loll against the bucking of the craft. The foreigner has found his place too, as easy as all of them. The day is clear but for clouds drifting far out to the west. They will build by mid-afternoon.

The boy casts his mind into the waters. Blue sailfish. His instinct is to cruise to the north, where there is a choice of three reefs. There, the cold Atlantic is infused by a geyser pumping hot minerals upward from two-hundred *faam* deep. There, krill gather, and plankton iridescent green on moonlit nights, and cruising sperm whales passing for the Arctic, and sailfish feasting on the mackerel that swirl through the rich deepwater current, and among them their king, the Blue.

Uncle Mike watches him, nodding approval at the choice of direction, at the clear plan.

'*Eat.*'

The boy sends his thoughts out into the cold waters, feeling as they bounce back to him against the shoals of mackerel, and the giant swellings of whale diving deeper.

'*Eat,*' moan the mackerel.

'*Hooom,*' pulses a grey whale with a calf at her side.

'*Et-et, et-et...*' shudder the dark creatures near the cold of the ocean floor. But no blue sailfish.

'*Eat!*'

This pulse is clear as day, as sharp as anger, and it comes directly from Uncle Mike's stabbing eyes.

The boy's arm sings a painful song. He keeps his hand tucked against his stomach as the leagues of ocean fall behind.

All the while the foreigner sits content in his lee from the wind, watching this open place with his seafaring eyes. Even though he is the outsider among them, he is the calm centre of the boat. The boy attempts to sound him but the man's mind is impenetrable. Again, he turns his attention to the sea. Land is gone from the horizon. All is blue and moving.

'*Eat.*'

Sailfish toward the eastern reef, three of them. More to the north but none of the size he seeks.

'*Eat.*'

'How reads the monitor?'

Mr Van Deventer has sent the words flinging over the heaving craft. The boy glances at the monitor, he has no interest in it, the screen is blank.

'*Nog niks* – still nothing,' he mutters, shaking his shaggy head.

And then it hits. He hears his quarry cruising at twenty *faam*, a giant among fish. She slides through the water, her great eye containing the world, and her great sail blue as the deep and streaked with green above her.

'*Tiiiinnnnngggggg...*' sings the mind of the fish, a lone and sustained note. She is not feeding.

The pain in the boy's arm disappears, the tension in his stomach evaporates. The hunt has begun. From now until its end, he and the fish will be one.

Van Deventer can see the change in the boy. 'What have you got?'

Hot adrenalin hits him. 'Good fish at twenty *faam*!' he shouts, the words falling awkwardly across his lip as he turns the boat to lay line and trail it across that broad beak. 'But she is not hungry, we must bait her. Lay line. Lay line!'

The boy's words ring with certainty. The men jump to, seizing their rods and flinging hooks with whole *cupper* sailing over the side as the *Sea Queen* begins her slow trawl.

The boy can hear the *cupper* fall, he can feel their fall echo through the waters, and the shift of the myriad life below him as they turn to it. He can smell the *cupper* in the water, as she can. A bull shark turns, nosing up for the bait, but the blue stays on course.

The boy watches the foreigner lolling against the bulkhead, watching the seven from behind his shades and, unknown to the boy, watching him also.

'She is not feeding. We must bait her.'

The boy steps out to the centre of the *Sea Queen*, easily riding her cant, and dances his way to the bulkhead.

'*Meneer*, have you got tails?'

He is pulling the anchor rope out of its hatch, searching behind it.

'What you want?' Van Deventer is watching him upside down, leaning back against the weight of his rod rising above him.

'Tails, sir. I'm sure you have some. We must bait her with some tails.'

The boy finds what he is looking for, a hessian sack still thick with the morning's muck and still cool in the bin of the anchor's hatch, and still crawling with life. He upends the sack to send a flood of tails flapping across the deck, young *kray* ticking and crawling at the touch of fresh air, all of them undersized.

The foreigner looks on.

'Hey!' Van Deventer does not like his secrets revealed.

'The fish is not hungry sir. She will eat when she tastes this.'

The boy stomps one of them across its still forming shell, crushing brain and carapace, sending crab fingers ticking. He stomps another, four of the pile, letting their muck and juice coat the others. He gathers them with both hands, the cracked bone in his right shoulder grating but unheard and unfelt, and scatters them over the side.

'He's lost his bloody mind!' Mostert is laughing, his rod arching above him. 'He's showing his colours.'

'*Just a boy, just a poor little boat-fishing boy who cannot afford even his own motor, or his own shirt.*'

'She is not hungry.'

The boy can see her in his mind's eye, cruising through the blue, her sail spread like a fan above, whispering through that deep, cold water. He watches, and then he smiles. For she turns, she has smelled the mess of shell and brain and meat, and she hears the flapping of those *kray* still living as they scoot through the deep, doomed with no shallow rock to claim as home. With a sweep of tail she turns, coming round, coming on to the line. A blue sailfish, as the boy knows, always has time for shellfish.

'*Eat*,' she murmurs.

Van Deventer is watching the boy, Uncle Mike is watching him too. Quietly, the foreigner looks on. He smiles with the joy of the sea. He knows a fisherman when he sees one.

'Be ready!' The boy returns to the wheel, full of that great fish. '*Eat*,' reverberates inside him.

'*Eat*,' she whispers as she comes closer. There the *cupper* hang, the mess of *kray* swirling around them, the strong nylon of the lines stretching through the blue.

There she comes, sailing through eternity.

CHIINNNG! pops fat Mostert's line, dipping hard enough to pull the man to his feet. His practiced hands fly to reel to release and let run. The fish sounds with *cupper* lodged in her throat. She shudders as hook cuts gill and pulls. She kicks.

'She is going to go all the way to the bottom. Then she is going to circle!'

The men watch the line spinning away.

'How much is on there?'

'Three-hundred *faam*,' says Mostert, letting it trail.

'I hope it's enough.'

'Sir, sir should tie off! Let her take our weight. The line is strong.'

'The boy's right. It's a fifty-kilo line. We'll drift with him, make the bastard tired.'

'I don't let boys tell me how to fish!' Mostert begins to work his rod once, twice, pumping it, letting the fish know she is in a fight, then releasing once again. The line sings off the reel, the fish dives deep dragging death with her.

'Theo. Don't be foolish. The boy is right. Better to keep him close, let him take our weight.'

Mostert shakes his head, his strong shoulders hunched over the rod in his fists. But he is a man of the cruel sea. He knows fish, he knows folly. He clicks his tongue, and flips the reel, bracing for the weight to come hard onto the rod.

GORRRK! The rod creaks and bends straight over, Mostert rising to make it a straight line into the foaming sea, taking any hint of tension he can off the creaking stick.

'Help me!'

Steel fingers and steel wrists steady him as the fish pulls him near the blue, pulling him back on deck, and bracing him there. With the faintest push, the craft takes a new course. Beneath them she pauses, feeling the tug of death doubled. And then she swims.

'It's a monster!' Van Deventer is staring at the reel in Mostert's fists. The boy glances at the foreigner. There is peace on his face. He rises to join them, he must, this is his sea also.

'It's a massive sonofabitch.' Mostert has clamped down on the rod, his fists steel claws. 'Now we wait him out.'

Quiet descends over the boat. The lapping of the ocean against the craft keeps them company, and the wheeling of two gulls, far from home and hoping for a meal.

For Mostert, pain begins, it is between him and the fish below.

For the boy, the pain of the fish begins. He feels the cutting steel in her mouth. He feels her strength, kicking against the weight looming above her.

'You are not afraid of the line breaking?'

This is the first time the foreigner has spoken. His words are accented and strange. Shyly, the men rearrange themselves. Van Deventer speaks for them.

'A fish of this size is older; he will take it slow. He is strong and experienced. He will not want to waste energy. This will tire him out. A younger fish, a smaller fish, he will want to jump and dive. We would give him line to hang himself with. A fish like this, we will drown him with our weight.'

The foreigner nods.

'How would you take him?' asks Mostert, not taking his eyes from the sea.

The foreigner considers the question; he looks up at the sun.

'Every fish is different. Even when you have him understood, he will surprise you. I like to catch with a lighter line, to make the catch more dangerous. But this is not preferred by my people. We will use a fixed line and a mechanical winch. We do not often use a rod any more.' He nods. 'I think you have a good way; I think you will catch a good fish.'

The men nod. His logic is their logic, the logic of the sea.

'You were using cloud-spinners on your boats when you caught your *tunny*, your tuna, last week.' Uncle Mike is talking, the sting of that day in his voice. 'We would not use cloud-spinners on *tunny*. We were surprised that you caught at all.'

'You would not?' The foreigner leans forward, genuinely interested. 'What would you use?'

'*Tunny* prefer bait at lower depth, or yellow *dollie*. They don't like metal; the sun flashes off it. They like sardine blood, and movement. But yellow *dollie* is their favourite.'

The foreigner nods, digesting the information.

'I'm sure you are right. We have not caught so well again. That day was but one.'

The men smile behind their moustaches. Pride is pride.

'In your country, you would use the spinner?'

'Yes.' He bows. 'Our *tunny*, our *sakana*, they do not mind the flashing of the sun. But there the sun does not rise so high, and it is not so bright. In my country the sea is not the same.'

'He's circling!' Mostert stands, bracing his thighs against the gunwale. Van Deventer and Nico Schaafsma stand too, their hands ready to grab. 'He does not like our hook!'

Mostert works the fish with constant pressure, making sure the hook remains jammed in her bony mouth. All can see that the fish is circling to the left.

The boy sits behind the wheel, his arms crossed at the chest, his eyes only half open. The pain in his arm pulses through him and blends with the pain in her jaw. They are indistinguishable. The boy breathes with gills as he sits at the wheel; he shimmers with scales. He follows the fish in his mind's eye, unaware that all the while, the foreign man, Mr Yoguchi, has one eye on him also.

Two-hundred *faam* down the great fish comes round, a puff of red trailing from her.

'Slack line!' yells Mostert, frantically working the reel.

'She's coming up!' The boy has jumped out of his trance. He drops the lever at his right hand, kicking the boat into reverse.

'*Wat maak hy?* What's he doing? Tell that sonofabitch it's my fish!' Mostert's hand whirs, trying to take up the slack.

'Get off the controls!' Uncle Mike is shouting, embarrassed by his boy.

'She's coming up fast, she wants to throw the hook!' The boy can feel her rising, he can feel her desire. 'She's going to jump!' He wills the *Sea Queen* to reverse even faster and to keep tension on the line. With a strong shake of that great head the hook could fall free.

'It's my bloody' fish!' roars Mostert.

'Leave that!' shouts Uncle Mike, grabbing the boy by the tattered collar.

'There's it!' calls Van Deventer. A shadow of silver rising through the blue, her body three quarters the length of the *Sea Queen*. And then she bursts free. The men are silent as she arcs against the sky, her sail snapped taut and spread, her eye moving over them as she turns, the white of the line sailing with her.

'The hook is still *vas* – it's tight,' calls Mocke.

'She's going to dive! Give line!'

'No, I have him now!'

'Line, give line!'

Mostert fumbles on the reel and, at the moment of pressure, his finger slips on the catch, so that he does not give line, and instead the falling fish pulls the line to breaking and Mocke, his hands numb from the long fight, does not let go. With a thump the line parts and the great fish falls free.

In a flash the boy is up on the gunwale on dancing feet, and in another he hefts a gaff in his left hand. The fish lies stunned on the surface, a boat's length from where they drift. He skips to bow, about to dive.

'No, no, no.' Van Deventer has his hand out and dug into the boy's tattered T-shirt. 'Come now, boy. That fish will cut you with one flick of its tail. A fair fight. He wins the day.'

Below them the fish turns, showing the silver of her side. Her great eye regards them, reflecting them all within it, before a shiver of her tail slips her beneath the surface, and with another she is gone. Around them the waters loom. It is just the *Sea Queen* and the men, alone.

'Fair fight, Mostert,' says Van Deventer, clapping his old friend on the shoulder. 'Fair fight.'

'Biggest fish I ever hooked,' Mostert says, stroking his beard.

'Fair fight,' says the foreigner.

The men slip into silence. For once, their thoughts are the same. Now, and later as they sigh into their beds, that great eye is with them.

CHAPTER EIGHT

By the time Jonothan returns to harbour his arm pulses and burns. From his shoulder to wrist it feels as if each throb will pull it from the socket. All day he has kept the pain hidden, during the hunt and the time after, when the men discussed the lost fish. And again, when they retired to the *cupper* grounds nearer inshore and caught their fill for dinner. Despite the loss of the great fish, as they snagged an afternoon's catch flapping from the cold, their bond grew. By day's end, when the boy brought the *Sea Queen* bobbing alongside the quay, there was a camaraderie among them. For all of them were true sea men, and somewhere inside there was relief to have touched that great creature but not to have robbed the world of it.

All the while the boy's pain had grown. He had refused a lift from Uncle Mike, staring him down, and he had remained respectfully quiet, acting the dumb boy when Van Deventer had realised the monitor had not been plugged in and wanted answers as to how the boy had guided them to both the Blue and a good school of *cupper*.

'How did you know the fish was there?'

'With the monitor, sir.'

'This thing's not plugged in!'

'It was on, *meneer*, of course it was.'

But during the long walk on that long dirt road, with his toes crunching upon the day's heat in the sand, he had finally dropped the mask and then the pain had come. The memory of Uncle Mike towering over him, and the smash of the stick into his flesh and the tearing of his arm, and the hatred he had felt, and the fear.

And so instead of turning toward his hut as he has done every night of his life, he finds his feet carrying him another way. The bay beckons, the cold of the ocean, and her.

As the sun draws the curtain on another day in a blaze of pink and orange, he crests the dune to the beach and stumbles into the cold, gasping as the water takes his arm, and his weight, and the pain, and covers it with ice.

He walks until the bottom gives way and the ocean begins to wash against his upturned chin, and then he swims ahead with three limbs, dragging the fourth behind. He wants to know where she is, he wants her beauty to burn the pain of this day away.

He wonders as he treads water out there, tiring under the weight of his trousers and his tattered shirt and most of all the cold that sucks at his bones and his lungs, inviting him under.

'*Where are you?*'

He remembers when he left her. He sees with a new jolt of pain the hurt in her eyes. This pain eclipses the pain of torn bone and ligament. What else could he do?

'*Where are you?*'

He knows that she will not come for him. He has known it always. Beings like her are not for his kind. His broken kind is for toil. He knows that he has betrayed his kind in thinking that his toil could be gone, in hoping that something as beautiful as she might be for him. He smiles, remembering the shape of his old self. The resignation, the knowing that life is this, that days are this toil forever and always. He puts his uninjured hand up to his face, allowing his fingers to explore the ridges of his lip, that sneering scar beneath his sparse beard. In that puckered and malformed skin that he knows so well, those peaks and valleys his fingers know so well, he feels the truth he cannot escape from. He is not for her. He is for no one.

She is not coming.

He rolls onto his back. He wants to be with the stars when his strength fails him, he wants to remember his one triumph, the blue sailfish and the look on fat Mostert's face when the great fish did come onto the line, did sound when he said it would, and did breach and sail above them with line arcing in the sun, as he said it would. He wants to bask in the beauty of that moment rather than the collapsed ridges of his own thoughts, his stupid face. 'I beat him today,' he whispers to Venus, who has unveiled herself down close to the horizon. 'He did not own me today.' Sirius appears winking above him, the brightest one of them all, and with it the belt of Orion and Betelgeuse, and the Seven Sisters, ready to hunt them again.

'He could not touch me,' he giggles as the cold steals into him, numbing his feet, clouding the pain in his arm, and whispering at his heart. 'Even though he broke my bone, he couldn't touch me.'

'I didn't let him find her,' he murmurs to Venus, her beauty intensifying as the sky slips from purple to black. 'He got nothing. She is still free.'

Gently he closes his eyes, ready to slip beneath the swell, ready to sleep, holding the image of her smile. He imagines her warmth, he lets it surround him. He knows she will not come. He abandoned her; he could do nothing else. He remembers the fear on her face. He closes his eyes, ready to forget.

'*My love.*'

Her voice in the darkness, threading through the cold.

'*My love. Wake up.*'

Again, he opens his eyes, looking up to Venus. My love. He giggles.

'*My love.*'

He blinks. '*My love?*'

'*Jonothan, wake up!*'

A shaking. The world is shaking.

'*Wake up! Wake up!*'

He opens his eyes fully, back to this world. The stars burn, brilliant in a swathe across the black sky.

'*Wake up!*'

He moans. '*I came to find you.*'

'*You are hurt.*' Her arms swirl about him, her hands, her fingertips, gently touching his injury. '*You are freezing.*' Her fin about him, her heat filling him.

'*I didn't want to wait until tomorrow.*' His eyes snap open. Cold returns. He groans at his arm.

'*What did he do to you?*' Her hands clasp his arm and her warmth invades it, dispelling the pain. '*What happened?*'

'*My love.*'

He laughs as he wakes fully and puts his arm around her shoulders. She doesn't answer. Her face is a mask of worry as she enfolds his shoulder with her fingers. Through the cold, he hisses at the pain.

'*You should not have gone with him.*'

'*He never found you.*' He mutters this, the dark returning.

'*Sssh.*'

His head falls to her collarbone.

'*Sssh*' as she fills him with all the warmth of her lonely heart. '*The water is cold, when you are gone.*'

She turns his head and places her mouth on his. She breathes into him, and together they slip beneath the swell.

Beneath the surface, in her cave past her guardian at the northern channel's head, she cradles him. Clams line the walls. In their centre she sits with him, the room pulsing with her warmth.

'*I'm sorry I left you.*'

She ministers to him, her hands weaving about the break in his shoulder.

'*I beat him today.*'

Beneath her fingertips the jagged pain of the break is smoothing, the bruised flesh relaxing, dark bruises draining away.

'*I did everything right. If Mr Mostert had listened to me, the biggest sailfish ever caught in the Baai would have been ours.*'

She can see all of it. The foreigner watching him as he felt the fish below, Mostert's shouts as the great fish sailed above them, her white belly as she finally turned and finned away.

'*I showed them. It's because of you.*'

He looks up at her then. Her hair swirls about the green of her eyes. She leans down and breathes into him. The taste of her on his tongue. Oxygen surges through his veins. Down in the cold of her cave he is on fire.

'*I had to leave you. I did not want him to find you.*'

And now, as he threads his fingers through the hair at the nape of her neck, it is his turn to see the day through her eyes: all of the hours since he left her, her solitude and the empty ocean yawning about her. For a moment he feels the vast waters as they were for her, without centre, nothing but the eternal current. He feels her loneliness.

She smiles at his thought. Her fingertips circling slowly about his shoulder. '*You exaggerate. This is my home.*'

In her smile he sees the truth of her words. She breathes into him again.

'*I wish I could be a fish. I wish I could be here, with you.*'

She stares into his beautiful eyes, taking all of him in. And then she breathes into him once more. And their heat rises. And the future rises.

In the dark of the deep night the two of them enter the tunnel to the northern channel, both moving over the dark one. She touches him lightly as she passes, and he purrs. At the entrance the two lovers pause to gaze at each other, and touch lips, and laugh at their joy. It is then that they both hear it.

'*Eat.*'

Their eyes swivel to the surface. It is coming from there. It is a fish they do not know, an alien to these waters.

'*Eat.*' It is a harsh sound, relentless.

'*Where is it?*' Each is asking the other, alternately holding each other's gaze or looking round, up and out, searching.

'*Eat.*'

And both hear it. A metallic tapping, a man-made sting that bends through the dark water. Both turn to the rock behind them, and from above another tap strikes through the rocky mass. *Tap-tap. Tap-tap.*

'*Eat.*'

Above them, near the surface, a new sight and a new sound. White light flashes, off and on, and with it the cyclical whoosh of artificial breathing. Instinctively they clasp hands and shrink back to the rock, hiding themselves as fish do when a hunter passes above.

At the surface the creature reveals itself, a swollen body covered in rubber, festooned with mask and breathing tank and diver's belt and swinging torch, and in the right hand a rod stretching out, barbed at the tip.

Uncle Mike fins lazily at the surface, every so often stopping to tap at Sentinel Rock with his spear gun, listening, and then beaming his torch to the rock and down to the ocean floor, his head obscured by his breathing bubbles.

The boy's heart hammers. He is shocked to see his tormentor so close, so near to their sacred place.

'*What is he doing here?*'

The boy's eyes widen with terror, his lungs suddenly heaving. She clasps his arm tighter, her own heart hammering at the shock of the floating thing.

'*My love.*' She attempts to reassure him, but she is too late. Panic is in his eyes. Bubbles escape his lips, rising in a column. Immediately that festooned head above snaps round, and the cruel light of its torch comes scything after. Behind them a new surging in the water. The dark one has awakened at the spreading panic. The boy feels the beast slither.

'*My love,*' she whispers, attempting to soothe his heart. '*My love.*'

But he is no fish and his calm down here is precarious. Suddenly his lungs are pumping in his chest and his mind is overtaken. Suddenly the threat above and the menace behind are nothing compared to his longing for air. He tears himself away from her, kicking up to the heavens just as the torchlight catches them both and she flits into the shadows. Uncle Mike looses his spear that comes rushing towards them. The boy rises free from the hole, kicking upward, pumping with all his might.

The surface is above him, an eternity away as he reaches upward, clawing for it, and suddenly he breaks free and breathes mightily. The stars greet his gulping face and his bulging eyes. Impassive, they twinkle above him. He drinks the night's cold air, treading water, as without her the cold of the sea returns. Quickly he looks down, plunging his face back through the veil and with maskless eyes he sees a boiling cloud down there, a wild swinging of the torchlight, and a mist of red rising up. Desperately he fills his lungs, filling his eyes with the stars before he upends himself and swims down, kicking and pulling at the water sliding through his fingers. He is not halfway when his panicked lungs begin to pump again and he must turn around, turn away. That last distance is impossible. All he sees is rising red and cascading bubbles, and the boiling form of Uncle Mike. He kicks upwards, desperate for the touch of the cold night on his lips.

'*My love!*' he shouts. '*My love!*' But he hears nothing but the sawing of his breathing.

He turns to lie on his back on the surface. He wills himself to calm, his heart to slow, as he begins to gulp air regularly, wanting to find the lungful and the calm he will need to reach the bottom.

'*Give me strength*,' he whispers to the three twinkling stars of Orion's Belt above. He is about to turn his face to the cold to try again when his body jerks to an impact at his ankle. With fearful strength he is dragged back into the northern channel, away from the cave. He cannot resist. He kicks with his numbed limbs but there is no movement in the biting cold. Sentinel Rock draws away from him, and before him on the surface swims the great form of Uncle Mike. His yellow scuba tank has breached the surface, his snorkel is a lonely finger pointing to the sky. In his wake is blood. The boy can taste it.

Dread seizes him. Despair like nothing he has ever known steals into his heart. All fight drains from him. She is dead, and so he is dead also.

Beyond that pointing snorkel drifts a small boat at anchor, a single white pilot light burning. Uncle Mike fins toward it.

Soon they have reached it and the boy will not respond. He lies dead in the water as Uncle Mike heaves him into the bottom of the boat. His face crunches against the wood and his body shivers with cold. He lies there, nailed to the bottom by grief, a stake of it buried in his heart.

'My love,' he moans. 'My love.'

He feels the wild rocking of the boat as Uncle Mike hauls himself into it, the clatter of streaming water hitting the deck, and the thudding of his tank and diver's belt as he shrugs them off.

Hatred rises in his heart. A cold fury. A clear intent. He opens his eyes. The boat tilts and the gear rolls towards him. Tied to the diver's belt he sees Uncle Mike's blade, inches from his face, the bright silver dulled by blood.

Hatred.

His breath hisses through his teeth as he prepares to shift and free his right hand, and reach for the knife. Certainty takes him and he sees the act clearly; his turn and thrusting upwards into Uncle Mike's bulging belly, and even as the big man's arms reach down to crush him, even as those fists bash his skull, he will twist the blade and slice it upwards, his last sensation the spilling of that gut. He readies himself for the movement, he is about to pull his hand free, when a sudden dead weight crushes him.

He gasps at the pressure on his lungs. The weight slides over him, pulsating haphazardly, twitching. Blood leaks into his mouth, and despair overwhelms him. It is her body on top of him. He opens his eyes, ready to look on her devastation. But in front of his face is a dark finger, spasming rhythmically, curling and uncurling in the aftermath of death, a finger with a swathe of sucker pads wiped across its edge. *The dark one.*

He licks his lips. Ink. Not blood. The flesh of a cephalopod, the twitching of a mollusk. Not her. Never her. She is not in this boat with them. He knows this suddenly. She is still in the water below.

He begins to laugh, the tiniest of chuckles bubbling through the twisting pile of the octopus as Uncle Mike primes his motor, one, two, and yanks it to life.

Braaauuup! Smoothly the dinghy turns in its moonlit wake, heading for the beach.

Thirty minutes later Uncle Mike has the beach in sight. It shines white beneath the slender moon, and the surf froths white at the sand. He aims his boat for the landing zone, cutting the motor as a wave raises them up and he coasts in on it. Beneath him the boat is filled with a carcass, a head and beak atop a pile of lifeless tentacles.

Uncle Mike wrinkles his nose in disgust. He did not expect to find that thing down there, a cephalapod of that size this far inshore. But he had dispatched it all the same, in the midst of its angry cloud of ink, its beak snapping at his face mask and its tentacles covering him with their sinuous power, while his knife slipped easily into the mantle and reached high, obliterating the heart. He had seen what he needed to, in the flashes of his torchlight swinging amongst the dying animal: a cave painted in clams. Pearl-bearing clams. He will harvest them.

That the boy appeared on the surface surprised him not at all. He has long since given up attempting to understand his strange mind. It is the boy's obsession with the northern channel that led him here, and the boy's discovery of the pearl.

He smiles to himself as he leans forward, bracing for the crunch of hull on sand, his little motor raised and stowed out of the water. The boy has finally delivered something useful.

He leaps from the boat and surges alongside it in the calf-deep surf, clamping a massive hand on the bow and pulling the boat up the beach.

'Serves the little bastard right,' he muses, eyeing the mass of cephalapod congealed and full of slime, knowing the boy is beneath it. 'He will have had a bumpy ride.'

Uncle Mike reaches his thick hand into the mess, pulling the ruined trunk and four of the tentacles with it. They slither and plop onto the sand. 'The boy can harvest this later,' he mutters. 'Good for the restaurant at the hotel, or to Van Deventer for *meel*.'

Uncle Mike reaches in further, grasping another tentacle that convulses at his touch, turning in the night air as he swings it from the boat, revealing the boy beneath. 'Asleep,' mutters Uncle Mike. 'Always asleep.'

He reaches in again for another handful, and the boy explodes into life. A blade flashes between them and Uncle Mike jumps back.

'You!' spits the boy. '*You!*'

Uncle Mike watches him, the boy's intent clear.

'You!' The boy hisses again, his face a mask of dark ink, his hair matted and clotted.

Suddenly the strike, faster than Uncle Mike expected, and surer too. The sting on the inside of his forearm as blade bites to the bone. He jerks away, his right hand to the wound as new blood wells between his fingers.

'What do you want, boy?' He can feel his blood pumping, he knows the cut is deep.

The boy stands erect before him, his eyes blazing beneath the waning moon, the blade held straight out between them. 'No more,' he whispers between clenched teeth, the words limping through his broken lips. 'No more.'

A moment longer he stands with the blade out towards the bigger man, and it takes a moment more for each to record what is before them: man, and across from him a boy, whose fierce eyes demand that time be halted and his vow remembered.

'No more,' says the boy, before the violence leaves him and in one movement he turns and begins to run down the beach, a single line of moonlit footprints laid in the sand.

Uncle Mike watches. The boy's form merges with the dark until there is nothing but the white curve of the beach and the curling of the white surf endlessly rolling onto it.

'No more,' Uncle Mike whispers to the now empty beach. 'No more.'

He sighs.

He looks down to his arm and the glistening blood. He removes his hand to let the mouth of the wound fall open, letting it bleed. He nods to himself. 'No more.'

PART II

CHAPTER NINE

Uncle Mike walks the sandy path with the carcass of the cephalopod piled high on his shoulders. The tentacles of the creature trail behind him, as does a trail of blood. Looking up Uncle Mike sees wisps of cloud swirl low against the distant light of the stars, and the faint glow of the moon. He can feel the weakness in him. He knows he is losing too much blood.

He grunts, irritated, as he turns his feet in a new direction, tracking not to his waiting vehicle but rather to the boy's hut. He knows the boy will have gut and needle there, and water for boiling. It angers him. He does not want to go to that hut.

He thinks about the boy: those fierce eyes that regarded him over the bloodied knife. 'Good,' he nods to himself. 'He has found his pride.'

As the blood flows from his open arm and the tentacles of the cephalopod collect muck and stone, the boy's hut rises into view.

Fresh irritation clouds him. The vegetable garden has gone to ruin. The apple tree stands wizened, what grass there was is a distant memory on this pile of sand. He grunts as he heaves the rubbery carcass off his shoulders and creaks open the door, his blood splashing on boot and stone.

He moves through the hut. Sure hands find matches in the dark, in their place next to the burner. He twists the valve and the flame burns high. He finds the pot where he knows it will be, and places it to boil. He searches in the free-standing cupboard next to the burner. His fingers rummage for gut and needle and other items he knows to be there. He finds the spool of thread, a booklet of needles, and then the twist of gut. He grunts. Nothing is new. The boy in all his years living here has added nothing. He sighs again. That boy.

He dips a cloth into the now boiling water, letting the heat soak through, and then sponges the open wound. His face does not flicker as the cloth drags the lips apart and the hot water probes inside. He takes iodine from the cupboard and splashes it into the meat, and then by the light of the burner he mends the wound with lines of gut, finally tying it off in a mess with his teeth and clipping it down. He places a match in the fire and burns the ragged ends away. He looks at the work. The wound throbs, but it is clean.

He reaches out and kills the burner. In the sudden dark an image lays itself across his eyes. Clams. A wall of them, like scales rising along the sloping rock. He sees again the swirl of ink, and the boy's panicked face as he rose past him. *What was he doing down there?* He shakes his head and lies down exhausted on the boy's stinking mattress. That the boy might return does not bother him. Sleep is what he needs, and he lets himself drift down.

He sleeps deeply. The night's dreaming covers him as his body does its work of healing. It is near dawn when his consciousness returns. The throbbing of his arm replaces his visions, and with it a sound he cannot place. Something is not right. His eyes flick open.

He listens carefully. The night's sounds are all around. Over the dune the surf booms and hisses, and a lone guineafowl cries in the veld. But no, it is nearer. And then he hears it again. A ragged breathing.

His eyes adjust to the near blackness of the hut. The moon has set, and the gloom is thick, but a little light bleeds from the stars, and slowly the shape of the door coalesces. It is ajar. He remembers that he had closed it. He raises himself to an elbow and reaches out in the darkness. His fingers find a length of wood, the boy's, kept near at hand for the times when baboons visit from the hills searching for plucked fruit, and fish, patiently raising the window latch or working the door handle. There is that sound again, that ragged breathing.

The darkness recedes as his pupils dilate, and then he sees it, lying just beyond the door. He grips the wood tighter, raising himself and then pausing once again. His nostrils flare. Warm blood.

The pile near the door is unmoving. A monkey, he thinks, attacked by one of the rare leopards still stalking the hills, a desperate animal that has clawed its way inside to die. He creeps nearer, ready for the creature to make a last stand.

The breath saws in the animal's throat, and then a sound that stops him cold. A voice.

He pads nearer, lowering the piece of wood, as the creature continues to call. It seems to be calling him. The voice makes no words; it is a voice that does not know words. The voice of an animal emerging from a human throat. It croons. It seems to be singing. He sees a hand rise in the darkness.

He reaches across to the little counter and takes up the boy's matches. Setting the wood down he strikes a match.

He sees hair dark as kelp, and green eyes bright with pain.

The creature is blinded by the flame; it cannot see what holds the match. Its mouth tugs into a smile beneath blood streaked across its face, and the hand opens to him.

The flame puffs out, but the image is burned to his mind. A girl lost in the veld and attacked by dogs? There is blood and dirt and below her waist a mess of ripped flesh.

Again, that strangled voice calling to him.

'Alright now,' he rumbles, carefully putting a massive hand to her shoulder. 'You will be okay now, don't fret now.'

The creature is suddenly still. No sound but that of the quiet night, and then she is fury. She explodes at him, fingers raking his eyes and chest, searching for anything to injure.

'Whoa now!' He clamps his hand about its neck, stretching his arm out so that it cannot reach his face. The creature boils and hisses, and suddenly screams. The fight goes out of it as a contraction grips her body. The mess of her legs writhe in the darkness.

'What is it?' he rumbles above her, 'what has happened?'

She screams again, her body peeling apart.

He stands, trying to take her in his arms to the sleeping mat. But she thrashes against him, raking his face and shoulders, her wild fingers catching the gut of his wound and ripping it open. He holds her as she flails.

Enfolding her so that she cannot strike he lowers her onto the mat, keeping his body close. Now he lets her go, stepping aside, and this time he moves to the gas burner, which he lights. He beholds her again. Her face is furious as she watches him, her chest heaving, running with blood, and below a mangled mess. Once again a contraction takes her. She drops her head back and screams.

Uncle Mike lifts the burner from the counter to light the girl better. He sees now, her legs are not as he imagined, the injury is not as he imagined. As he moves about her and she screams so the light moves also, chasing the dark from her legs. He comes to her feet and crouches down, mesmerised by what he sees. There are not two mangled feet before him, as he had imagined; instead he sees a tail ridged with fin, the fan spread on the dusty floor. It is slashed and battered, dragged across rock.

She is screaming at him, unable to move for the pain that wracks her, and then another spasm hits. Her wild eyes leave his, instead raised skywards. In her scream the tail undulates, and then a slit forms down the middle. Fresh blood leaks to the floor. Something is emerging in the flickering light.

She reaches up to push his face away, she does not want him to look at her. But she cannot rise. She is pinned down. He pays her no mind; instead, he watches. She screams once more, a final cry, as the flesh of the tail fully sloughs away. And with a final gasp, she loses consciousness.

He sits in the flickering dark with the creature asleep before him. He cannot believe his eyes. Twin gills slit across her neck, but she does not seem to use them. Her pale mouth is open as she breathes. The mass of her hair circles her head and snakes down her chest. Her navel is concave and ridged where the hard muscle of what was her tail twists up into her ribcage and around to her spine. She is a powerful fish, he can see, her torso and hips made for swimming. Below her navel is the miracle. Here is a mess of crusted blood. It has collected and scabbed around her hairless groin, streaked across two legs that lie curled to the side. The remnants of her tail lie beneath her. He leans forward to look closer. Nestled in the muck of the discarded tail are two perfect feet, two ankles, two knees. He cannot believe what he sees, and yet here she lies. The night provides no answers.

He takes hold of the tail. He traces it with his fingers, a fan similar to the dorsal fin of the sail fish. It is cold now, and congealing. He pulls it from beneath her, watching for her to wake, but she is lost to sleep. He folds the meat together and places it aside.

He has boiled water and has a bucket beside him. He begins to sponge the blood from her, fascinated as the gore falls away. She is a girl but not a girl. She is a fish but not a fish. Her legs remind him of the fresh bud of an octopus tentacle that has formed to replace one lost. Soft still; they are growing.

On his haunches he moves about her, examining all in detail. Her groin is human, her torso smooth and ridged with muscle. Her arms are as a human's, her fingers webbed. A girl but not a girl, a fish but not a fish.

'Strange fish,' he mutters, as he traces her joints with his fingers, as he opens her mouth to peer into her gill-slitted throat. He strokes the now dry mat of her hair away from her face. He traces the lines of cheeks and jaw. He puts his face close to her skin, peering at it. It is completely smooth; there are no pores. He touches and realises the skin is dry. He lifts her arm and wipes the pad of his thumb across her hairless armpit. Dry also. She will not sweat.

'You will find it hard here, under the sun,' he murmurs, as he stands and goes to the cupboard. He takes a jar of lard and kneels down again. He dips his hand in the lard and begins to massage it into the flesh. He works steadily, covering all of her body with the thick ointment. He takes extra time with her legs, kneading and discovering every sinew and muscle and bone within. He takes time to coat all of her: her neck, her shoulders and her back, her arms and elbows, her wrists and hands, her chest and stomach, her groin, her thighs, down and down to the ends of her toes. As the night fades to morning, so he covers all of her and touches all of her and casts an impression of her that takes root in his own bones. Finally he notices day's soft light stealing into the cabin. Stiffly, he stands.

Once again he looks down at her.

He pulls the soiled blankets away and into them he places her fin. He moves outside where the air is still cold and raises gooseflesh on his skin. He pads to the tanks behind the hut. He places his bundle upon the hard ground. From a collection of tools leaning beside the hut he hefts a pick. He turns to the tree spreading above him. He remembers when this plant was full with bursting green leaf and apples hanging low. He sees how barren they are now, sprouting nothing but hard fists of fruit that wither too soon. This tree, as the sea, is dying. He turns to the ground and begins to dig. Dust and dry dirt rises.

As the sun begins to crest over the faraway hills, he steps away. There is a hole in the turned earth. He collects the bundle with the tail and stands before the coming sun. In the growing light he inspects it also. It is like no tail he has ever seen. There are no scales, like a dolphin, and yet the fan is fibrous, like a fish. He is about to cover it when the sun crests. First light strikes the flesh in his hands and for a moment colour explodes through it. He has seen such patterning before. It is the colour running through a mollusc as it camouflages itself on the sea bed. Colour pulses in the meat, and then it is gone. So too is the first moment of morning. Already he can feel the sun's heat and now the tail in his hands is heavy and dull, soon to stink. He kneels and places the bundle in the ground. With the pick he fills the hole and places rocks above it, forming a cairn.

Quickly he washes himself in the boy's water tank and then goes inside.

There, from the clutter of the boy's tools, he selects a length of wire. He kneels, taking up the still sleeping creature's wrists, and binds the wire around them. He attaches rope to the wire and ties that to the cupboard. He looks on her a moment more, and then turns to the little door. He has much to do in the world, this day.

She moans. All is heat. Her skin is fire. The harsh weave of the blanket scratches. Her eyes not yet open, she throws the blanket aside. Sharp pain immediately burns at her wrists. She opens her eyes to see them bound and a rope snaking from them to the cupboard nearby.

She pulls at the rope. She remembers. *Him.*

And then: '*Where is Jono?*'

The night floods back. Her face creases into a snarl. She pulls at her chains, jerking with all her strength, but the cupboard is nailed to the floor. Wire cuts into her wrists. She pants, and then catches sight of them. Peeking out from the blanket covering her are two feet. The toes move. *Her* toes. She shifts the blanket to reveal two ankles. She shifts the blanket again, and two shins and two knees emerge, and finally two thighs stretching from her hips. She pulls the blanket aside and regards herself. This new body. She turns her head and regards the hut. This new world. Again she looks down to her wrists. *This new world.*

On her hands and knees she leaves the sleeping mat, dragging her new legs behind her as she explores the hut, moving as far as the rope will allow. She examines the burner, and Jono's simple utensils, and the drawers of the cupboard that slide open and closed, and everything of him that speaks of him, and of his absence.

Where is he?

She turns to the door, now closed, and the small window next to it. The world is out there. Her love is out there. He must be. She looks through the window to the sky – a brilliant day out there – and she listens to the distant boom of surf, and home. She cranes her head to see more, and something catches her eye. A dark thing hanging. She crawls further toward the door, aware that her rope is running out. Soon it is tight and she leaves her wrist behind as she stretches her arms backward and forward, her hand reaching for the door handle.

It does not open easily. First she must discover the mechanism, the need to pull it down, and the need to bump against the door long swollen in its frame, but finally she swings it open. She goes cold. Hung on the beams on which old netting brings shade from the sun is the cephalopod. It is strung up, tentacles stretching away from the great head and beak in the centre, eyes shrivelled and putrefying in their sockets. She sees the violence of the missing tentacles, harsh wounds left open to the sun, and feels the frenzy in which it must have died. She covers her eyes. Her dark one.

She sits, unable to look, until she forces herself to. Her chin rises up, pointing to the carcass. Carefully she uses the door handle to pull herself onto her rubbery legs. She stands teetering against the door. Her eyes meet the ruined head, and a fury builds in her. She lets it rise, filling every cell, coating her new legs with intent. She turns, fixing her eyes on the cupboard, and slowly takes her first step toward it. Her hands leave the door handle and there she trembles, until she steps again, and just before she falls, she reaches the cupboard with hands outstretched. *There*. She leans against it.

She knows she is alone. Jono cannot be here. Something must have happened. Again her knuckles clench white and she rises, and turns, and makes her way back to the door. This time she walks with a new intent. She reaches the doorway and again regards the ruined head. Taking another step forward so that she balances against the taut rope, she reaches out with her free hand. She touches the cheek of the cephalopod, stroking it for a moment, before slipping her hand inside the beak. At the limit of her reach she finds what she is looking for. Beneath her fingers she feels something sharp and unyielding. Carefully she grasps it and pulls against the softening flesh. Slowly, the prize comes to her. Slowly, determination rises in her eyes.

At the head of the northern channel, Uncle Mike bobs on the waves. He is atop his *fabriek*'s vessel, the *Elizabeth*, and with him are men that Salie has brought from the settlement near the town. These are men that know how to dive deep and quick into the cold waters, taking scuttling *kray* from beneath rock and spiriting them away before the conservation officers appear.

These are the right men for the job.

Dressed in their own dark rubber they eye the bulk of Uncle Mike. These are men who, if necessary, will bring a blade into the sunlight and flick it quickly into flesh, and even they watch him warily. The man is legendary in the Baai.

'Tell them that no one is to open a clam,' Uncle Mike grunts to Salie, looking not at the men but rather at the finger of Sentinel Rock rising above him.

'No one is to open a clam,' says Salie to the men waiting. 'We bring all the clams to the surface, and all of them stay closed. *Reg so*? Is that right?'

The men grin and bob their heads on the bobbing boat. '*Ja*, Salie, *reg so* – that's okay.' They giggle. 'We will not touch your clams.'

'They better not,' mutters Mike.

'You better not,' smiles Salie.

The men hear and smile also. They know that a blade can always do work.

'Come then,' says Uncle Mike. He places his mask over his face and his regulator into his mouth and turns and falls into the green. He begins to fin down to the tunnel at the base of the Sentinel. He will allow the men to strip the clams and he will remain at the entrance ensuring that every one is passed back to the surface, and passed whole.

He enters the tunnel, cautious of the possibility of another cephalopod, even though he knows the chance of two in one burrow is slim. Again he glimpses the interior of the cave through weed as he glides through; again he sees that wall of concentric shells rising. He enters the cave and pauses, because he must. Not only are the walls thick with clam, but the floor also, every inch of rock covered in the spheres of these shells as they rise to the chimney and a small breathing space up there. Their uniformity is such that the walls seem smooth, a strange concentric beauty that shimmers in dappled light.

Uncle Mike motions to the left and right. The men fan out to the walls and to the floor and begin their practiced work. Chisels quickly and efficiently shuck shell from rock, and clams disappear into netted bags. As the men begin to wipe the clams from the walls, as the beauty of this place begins to crumble, so Uncle Mike looks up to the flume above and the sun.

'*How can she be?*'

He contents himself to sit quietly at the entrance to this cave while the men do their work, watching, waiting, and wondering at the splendid thing that even now sleeps in the boy's hut.

The deck of the *Elizabeth* is strewn with black clams.

'Have you seen clams like these?' Uncle Mike asks Salie, who holds one in his fist.

'I haven't,' says Salie, shaking his head. The little man turns the big clam over. As he does so colour bursts through the black calcite, causing a wave of blues and pinks. He squats down to the deck and runs his hands through the pile of them. 'They are bigger than I have ever seen. And the colour...'

Uncle Mike eyes the men at the bow of the *Elizabeth* who are clustered around a burner on which a pot boils. They are making soup to warm them after their long dive. At their feet are their netting sacks. They too are ankle deep in clams.

'I don't want these men back with us tomorrow.'

Salie nods, his hands on the wheel of the *Elizabeth* as he turns them back towards the harbour.

'And I don't want the town knowing about our catch either. You can dock at the old jetty, take them straight to the *fabriek*. There I want you to store them in the tank for me. I want to keep them alive for now.'

'We can do that.'

'What will it take to keep these boys quiet?'

'They know our secrets, but we know theirs. In these days, with these foreigners stinking up the harbour, they are happy to have friends. They will get their pay, and they will be happy with it.'

Uncle Mike lays his hand on little Salie's shoulder. The bones beneath the frayed wool of his fishing jersey are light and brittle, but the eyes of the man are bright. He has been with Uncle Mike for twenty years. The bond between them is strong, and sealed by secrets.

Uncle Mike strides forward, his booted feet swishing through the clams strewn about the deck. The men watch him come. Their faces flicker not at all, but their hands are ready to reach to hidden pockets. He stops just a metre away.

'Salie will see to your pay. Thank you for your work today.'

'Thank you, *meneer.*'

'I will take these bags of yours. Salie will pay you for these also. A fair price.'

The men do not look to each other. Instead it is one among them that answers.

'Sure, boss.'

Uncle Mike nods to them before he bends and takes up their green net bags and begins to scoop clams into them. It is not long until every bag is bulging and tied and waiting beneath the gunwale.

'I want no one to know of these clams. Have you got me, Salie?'

'I have you boss. The Baai will not know of these clams.'

Uncle Mike nods. From the side of the wheelhouse he takes up a mottled old life preserver. It is orange streaked with the white, black and grey of seasons of birds passing over it.

'I will come and find you at the *fabriek* tomorrow.'

Uncle Mike threads his great arm through the life preserver, wedging it on the bulge of his shoulder. In his left hand he takes up the clutch of net bags swollen with their harvest, and hefts them, and goes to stand on the gunwale, and then launches himself into the green.

This time the men react. They jerk their heads as one to see the big man splash into the water and then surface with his face toward the sky. They watch with wide grins as he moves off to the distant line of the beach. His feet drive with powerful kicks leaving a wake behind him.

Salie smiles. The man has a swim of a kilometre in deep water ahead of him, dragging the weight of the clams. And he knows he will do it. All the men in the *Elizabeth* know he will do it.

'*Julle varke* – you pigs, leave that soup and get these clams packed in the hold. We will unload at the *fabriek* tonight, so you will have time for goofing off later. Work now my *varkies* – my little pigs – and Salie will have a fat present for each of your wallets tonight.'

The men do not yet move. They want to hold the image of Uncle Mike in the immensity of the water, and his wake stretching back towards them.

'*Varkies*!' barks Salie. 'Come!'

The men stand, the leader of them tapping off their burner so that the bubbling in their soup fades away.

'*Ja*, Captain!' They jump to the drifts of clams still spread across the deck. Swiftly under their hands the glittering shells are wiped into the hold, revealing the white painted deck beneath. Tonight the men will box their catch. Later, under the light of the moon, they will bring them quietly into the *fabriek*.

Uncle Mike looks to the sky. The cold of the Atlantic flows past his head and down his body, and the weight of the collected clams pulls at his left fist. The wound on his arm stings as the water washes through it. He does not mind the cold. He was born in cooler climes, and he still remembers the snow and ice; it is the sun and heat that causes him to frown. He is glad to be away from the *Elizabeth* and alone in the water. Now is the time to think.

As the cold water massages him, he casts his mind to the hut, where the creature is waiting. Will the boy return? He does not think so. He remembers the look in his eye as they faced each other over his blade. It was the look of finality. The boy is his own man now; he will be moving as far as he can from his old life. And the creature? It is obvious to Uncle Mike that she is the source of the boy's rebellion. He shakes his head as the water passes over his ears. A mermaid? These things do not exist. And yet in his fists he holds clams like none he has ever seen, and above him and all around him is a world that in all its pulsing life does not conform. Who can make sense of it? The creature is there, she is as real as the wire with which he has bound her.

He shakes his head in the water, shaking the vision of her from his eyes. He cannot dwell.

'Will the boy come back?'

As he poses the question to himself again he feels a tightening in his gut.

The boy is not the question, he tells himself, and neither is the creature. It is the gift of clams he has been given, in the face of the invasion of these foreigners. It is the gift of a new future that is important. This is where he must lay his intent.

Around him he feels the rising of the swell as the land rises beneath him, and so he turns onto his belly. Here is the beach, here are the rocks of the slipway he has known all these long years. He allows his feet to sink and find purchase in the sand. With his toes he pushes himself through the water, allowing his arm to rest a moment as he nears the rocks, and then he pushes off again to swim in under the shadow of boulders, shielding himself from the beach.

Can he trust that the boy will not return and take the creature? No, he cannot. Can he trust that Salie will keep his word and keep the clams on the *Elizabeth* secret? No, he cannot. Nor can he assume that Salie will control the loyalty of the men who assisted this morning. He regrets bringing them. It was in fact a job he could have handled on his own. However, in all of this uncertainty, he feels the solidity of the clams he now holds. These are his. These clams and this wild and deserted beach, he can trust.

He clambers out of the water onto the rocks. He threads his bags together and wedges their tail between one boulder and another, so that they lie submerged and hidden from all eyes. He secures them tightly, securing his own future and that of the Baai too, as he sees it.

He must take his chances with the creature – what she has to offer him he does not know. If the boy returns it is of no consequence – he has nothing to fear from him, and perhaps he can be of use. With Salie and the men he will play the game of survival that he has played with all others, and on which he has built his own *fabriek* among the seven in this Baai.

He passes out from the rocks carefully, watching the deserted beach, mindful of any eyes that may record him here. He sees none and feels none, and he jumps from rock to rock to avoid leaving his own wet prints in the sand. He makes his way to his little motor parked beneath the eucalyptus grove. He must follow his intent, and so he starts his motor and heads left on the silent tar, away from the hut.

As he drives, the hot, low mountains of the Baai float beside him, and those green eyes drift within. They wait for him every time he blinks.

Uncle Mike pulls in to the sun-swept courtyard of Mocke Fisheries Inc, a cluster of low buildings very like his own *fabriek*. He parks in the wide parade area before the main sorting hall and climbs out.

Mocke's is the oldest *fabriek* in the Baai, which is more in Mocke's blood that anyone else. Although he is not the leader of the seven owners (that title falls to Van Deventer and the mining money his grandfather brought with him fifty years before), Mocke is the counsel Uncle Mike is looking for today. Mocke is the voice of reason among a group with few ways left to turn.

Uncle Mike strides out into the sun reflecting bright off the concrete, angling for the big double doors of the main sorting hall and Mocke's tiny office, with its windows looking out at the moving conveyer belts.

'Mikey,' calls a voice behind him, and Uncle Mike turns to see Mocke shuffling towards him. The old man wears his habitual blue-and-white checked shirt; his jeans are thrust into strong work boots, and the brown leather braces he prefers snake over his shoulders. He carries a starter motor in his right hand. Behind him Uncle Mike can see his ancient Datsun 640 motor parked, with the bonnet up.

'Uncle Thys,' says Mike, holding out his big hand.

'Mikey,' says the hurried Mocke, shaking the offered paw as he passes and gestures for Uncle Mike to walk with him. 'Sorry, I'm struggling with that damn motor. Starter's buggered, looks like.'

Mocke shuffles into the cool of the big sorting hall. Uncle Mike follows, allowing his eyes to drift to sights he knows well. The lines of conveyer belt manned by rows of women, the stacks of pallets growing as two forklifts buzz between them, and the flow of day workers from the fish *meel* plant passing through.

'You've got some good stock,' says Uncle Mike, eyeing the stream of fish on the belts.

'Yes, some *tunny*. Caught by the foreigners, you remember? They can't process until their factory ship arrives. They have sent me some on consignment.'

'Looks fresh.' Uncle Mike reaches out to grab a tunny tail as the flecked-open fish pass between one woman and the next. 'They caught nearly a month ago.'

'Their fridges are no joke,' says Mocke, nodding, his steady shuffle taking them to an exit door on the far side of the floor.

Mocke turns left into a passageway running the length of the sorting floor. Just like Uncle Mike's *fabriek*, this is the entrance to the storage units ringing the main hall. Mocke heads straight on, ignoring the big refrigeration doors.

'So, you have been talking with Yoguchi?'

'Of course, Mikey. When a man comes into your harbour with boats that can sink your own, it's best to see what he wants. Don't you think?'

Uncle Mike nods grudgingly.

'What's he say about our offer?'

Mocke sighs and shakes his head. He stops, forcing the big man to stop with him. 'Hold this,' he says, passing him the grimy motor. Uncle Mike takes it as Mocke digs in his dirty denim pocket. He brings out a ring of muck-flecked keys, which he compares against the lock in front of him.

'Yoguchi doesn't think much of our offer. He knows we have nothing he doesn't already have, except our Baai.'

He selects a golden key from the clutch of silver and brown and slips it into the padlock. 'He's not interested in our crappy boats, but he is motivated to keep us as friends. So, he has offered me work for my people.'

Mocke cracks the old lock open and slips the bolt back, letting the old door swing on its hinges. He reaches in and flicks a switch to his right, flooding the little room with light from a dust-smeared bulb above them. Inside is a jumble. Shelves from floor to ceiling, each packed with spares collected over the years, all thick with grime. Mocke begins his search, trailing his hand in front of his eyes as he looks up and down the rows. 'I don't think we will get any kind of partnership with Yoguchi, but we will be able to feed ourselves with his crumbs.'

'I am not happy with crumbs.'

'No, you have never been that sort of man.'

Mocke picks a cobweb covered part from the jumble in front of him.

He turns it over in the light.

'And what do you mean by that?'

The old man glances up at Uncle Mike. 'Come now, Mikey, we all know you will rather fight than win.'

He holds the part up in front of him, an old starter motor. He takes hold of the tiny rusted flywheel, rotating it with his forefinger. He grunts and replaces the part to the shelf, again allowing his hand to drift along the jumble.

'I was taught to never submit.'

'You are a fighter...' Mocke allows the 'f' to sigh through his teeth, letting it hiss. 'We are not fighters; we are fishermen. We know when to drop our anchor. We don't try to sail against a storm.' Mocke chuckles, prodding the jumble in front of him.

'What if we left them to their fishing, what if we did something else?'

'Something else?'

'You used to farm with abalone. What happened to that?'

'My tanks are still here; bone dry under the sun. Abalone do not like living in tanks, I have discovered. They lie empty there at the back.'

Mocke takes hold of another machine. He lifts it and looks, another starter covered in dust. He holds the flywheel on its tip to his eye, rotating it. He turns and compares it against the one still held in Uncle Mike's fist. 'My little motor won't start because of this.' Mocke prods the old flywheel which wobbles on its axis. 'This little, broken wheel.'

He lifts the motor from Uncle Mike's hand and tosses it to the floor, kicking it to the dark of the lowest shelf. He turns to the doorway, clicking off the light as he goes. Uncle Mike follows him.

'Why, are you interested in farming?'

'I am interested in us keeping our Baai.'

'To keep a stretch of coastline. Now, that is a tricky thing.'

'This place is ours. We cannot let them take it over.'

'My family has been here for many years longer than any of you, than anyone here but the *strandlopers* – the beach walkers. They remember this place empty. The tide is the tide. It rises without us.'

Uncle Mike walks behind the old man, a lumbering giant forced into silence. Again they pass the lines of sorting women, descendants of those beach walkers. Their knives dart from fingers that could gut a fish in the dark, or spin a net into the world. Hands that remember a Baai before boat or sail.

'Yoguchi did have one thing to ask of us,' says Mocke after a time, when the two are halfway across the sorting floor. 'He wanted to know about that boy of yours. He thinks he is quite the fisherman.'

'He asked about him?'

'We all saw it – how he found that sailfish. Van Deventer swears his echo finder was not plugged in.'

Uncle Mike shrugs. 'The boy has a talent. It's not a surprise. Many are good with fish.'

'That boy is unexplainable.'

Uncle Mike does not answer.

'Why do you hate him so?'

Uncle Mike shakes his head.

'You are a difficult man, Mikey.'

'We are each as we are.'

The two stop before the open bonnet of Mocke's motor, held together by the man's care over the years. Mocke places his new starter on the rusted battery. With calloused fingers he takes a wire brush to the little flywheel. Dust and rust fly from it.

'I gave the boy every opportunity. I fed him and housed him, gave him work, the chance to fish. What more must I do?'

'You've treated him like an animal. Boys need more than food.'

Mocke reaches into the guts of the old car, putting his new motor in its slot and one by one placing nuts to screws. 'Where is he?'

'He does as he pleases.'

Mocke closes his eyes as his fingers tighten the last bolt. 'Yoguchi is looking for him. He will find him, eventually.'

Uncle Mike shakes his head in frustration. He will speak no more about it.

'All of your abalone gear. It's still out there?'

'Yes, as I said.'

'Can I have it?'

Mocke squints up to the man beside him. The sun is behind him now, making a shadow wreathed in orange and dancing white.

'What are you thinking, Mikey?'

'I just want to see what I can do. I don't much like the taste of crumbs.'

Mocke shrugs. 'Have a look. Anything you want, just clear it with Mr Saviours. He will know what we must keep. But I doubt it. It's all junk.'

'Are you really going to give this all to them?' Uncle Mike gestures to the sea.

Mocke straightens. 'This is no one's place,' he says, clicking the bonnet closed. 'Your people came from the mountains, your wife from over a foreign sea.' He looks out at the dark ocean spreading away from them. In the building wind the sea seems like concrete against the contour of the land. 'This is no one's place. The wind and the tide will wash us all away.'

'Thank you, *Oom*,' says Uncle Mike, holding out his hand.

Mocke takes it lightly, not taking his eyes from the big man's face.

'Give the boy some slack, Mikey. His mother is long gone.'

Again Uncle Mike shakes his head. Respectfully he turns from the older man.

He trudges back towards the sorting hall, but instead of entering he bears right, taking a path through the low bush.

The sound of the sorting hall is muffled by the empty refrigeration units. Out here is the sound of the wind, and the weight of the afternoon sun. He squints against the bright light as he walks through soft sand. He feels the weight of years.

Abruptly the main building to his left comes to an end. Behind it is open land, stretching down to the wind-brushed ocean. Three old tanks lie sealed in black tarp, their dry mouths open to the sun. Around them are the remnants of an industry: pumps fallen into disuse, cleaning nets and filtration equipment piled in drifts, all broken down.

Uncle Mike views the empty pits. He imagines them full of oxygenated water, covered with shade cloth and bursting with silver-shelled abalone. He hears Mocke's words: *You would rather fight than win.*

'No, old man, you do not know me at all,' he mutters, as he steps off the path and makes his way to the empty tanks.

It is nearing evening when Uncle Mike finally returns to Jonothan's hut. In the back of his motor he has packed all the gear tall Mr Saviours had allowed him to take. In the back he also has his netting bags tied shut under a cloth, full of black and whiskered clam. He stops the motor beside the little gate, and sits a moment in the cab, eyeing the hut. She will have been there all day.

All looks as it was: the hut perched on the veld beneath the colouring sky, the dark cephalopod strung up on the eaves and no doubt drying well. And the boy? He sees no sign of him. He shakes his grizzled head. The boy will return when he does, if he does.

He steps out of the motor and reaches into the load bed to grab his clams. He lifts them over the fence as he clicks through the gate and deposits them next to the workbench. He lumbers over to the little door. She is not in the kitchen; she must be at the sleeping mat just out of sight. He can see the rope he used to tie her to the standing cupboard. It trails away.

He takes the handle in his fist and pulls the door toward him. He ducks and steps inside. Yes, there she lies, on the mat. The late afternoon sun falls through the kitchen window onto her. She is uncovered, her new legs straight out in front of her, her hair smeared across her chest and the mat and floor beneath her. The rope trails from her wired wrists.

Uncle Mike drops to his haunches, studying her in the light of day. Every part of her is alien, and perfect.

But she is weak, he can see that too. The cuts all along her legs have scabbed, but they do not look healthy. He inches closer. Her skin is dry. It is as he suspected. She needs water. Despite this, her new legs have grown stronger. Muscle has bloomed in them, setting them.

'Do not worry,' he rumbles, looking down on her.

Her eyes spring open.

He pauses, the effect of them is startling.

'*Middag* – afternoon.'

She turns toward him. Without looking him in the eye, she studies him.

'I have brought you some food.'

He places two apples and a sandwich from the petrol station shop on the floor before her. 'Maybe you are hungry?'

She says nothing, watching him. Her eyes travel along his body, studying every part. He is suddenly uncomfortable, suddenly aware of her nakedness.

Her eyes travel along his torso, shifting across to his left arm, alighting on the wound that is now hidden beneath his sleeve. She watches the place and to his surprise he feels an itch bloom inside it. His eyes dart to hers, but she does not meet his gaze. She moves, folding her legs in front of her. She raises her hands still bound by the wire. With her right forefinger she points to the wound.

'*Come.*'

He hears the word inside him, her voice whispering to him without sound.

'*Let me see.*'

He finds himself walking towards her.

She opens all her fingers, waiting for his right arm.

'*Let me see.*'

He kneels down to her, looking into her green eyes, which still avoid him.

He rolls his sleeve up for her. The cut lies angry on his skin. The stitches are laid open. The wound is red, infection a whisper away. She places her hands on it. He gasps. A gentle warmth grows, easing the throbbing.

A smile passes over her lips. He watches it with wonder. This exquisite creature. But suddenly a foreboding fills him. There is something within her smile, a hard edge, a truth he cannot quite fathom. Suddenly her smile seems not a smile, but a snarl.

A faint growl fills the air. He hears it as one hears a voice of long ago, a voice in memory. He drops his eyes to his arm and there, in that slow space between thinking and movement, an object appears in her left hand. It is a sliver of black, the size of a beetle, and with a flick she moves it to the open wound.

'*Hagh!*'

His nervous system activates. He jerks his arm but her fingers hook into him, her body following him as that dark pearl of the cephalopod's poison sac touches the mouth of the wound.

Panic rises in him, and then fades to an unexpected calm. He knows the pain that is coming; he has seen the convulsions of a man stung by a cephalopod, but he does not care. He knows he will not try to escape. He looks to her eyes and for the first time he finds them staring back at him.

He shudders. They are the eyes of a predator, incongruous in her face, fathomless, deep and as uncaring as a trench. He braces for the agony, but the sting does not come.

He breathes.

The two regard each other, black iris to green.

This is the closest she has been to him, and he is not as she imagined. Peaks overhang the eyes, crags are riven in the cheeks. Where from a distance she saw cruelty, now she sees a new truth. Pain. His face is a mask of it. She cannot take her eyes from his. She reads all, she feels all. Grief sits heavy in this man. Grief like a lake frozen over.

She cannot help herself. She begins to dive into his mind, but he will not let her.

They breathe, looking deeply into each other.

She smiles, her teeth sharp.

And he smiles too.

'Do it,' he murmurs.

'*No.*' And her smile widens.

Her goal was to inflict pain, but instead she has found a creature writhing in it. The mountain that he is, is tumbling down, moment by moment, as he is eaten by grief within. This man is broken. Her revenge is playing out before her eyes. Death would simply make him whole.

'Do it,' he whispers again.

She pulls her hand away, the barb withdrawn.

'*Suffer rather.*'

The two regard each other anew. Truth has passed between them.

'You are cruel.'

She reaches up to touch his craggy face, fascinated.

As she traces the story across his face, so he marvels at her also. Exhaustion invades her suddenly, and gently she drops her hand and lies back on the mattress, her green eyes closing to sleep.

Uncle Mike sits cross-legged on the floor of the little hut. Next to him there is a drawer from the standing cupboard. He has pulled it out.

As she has slept he has once again rubbed her with lard. She is weak from lack of water, he knows, and he has covered her skin in water also, spending the day's last hours watching her skin shimmer in the golden light, as it drinks each drop he lets fall on her. She will need more of it, and so he has placed a bucket with cloth beside her. He takes her hand, swallowing it with his own.

'I wonder what kind of animal you are.'

Gently he places her hand on the floor, and then he reaches to the drawer next to him. It is packed tightly with clothing. Items long ago laundered and folded, and shut away. He lifts a garment from it. A cotton dress. He unfolds it above her and lays it out. It is her size.

Gently he slips the dress over her as she sleeps. Gently he smooths the dress down her body, the feel of cotton on her skin, the feel of memory.

He sits with her thus, his head bowed and his hands resting upon her sleeping body. His eyes close. He is grateful that she sleeps, he is grateful for the solitude of this hut.

He reaches into his pocket and with a click he raises his blade. She sleeps beneath the unfolded steel. He puts the blade to her wrist and teases the wire out, undoing his knot. Gently he unwinds it, and severs both.

He puts his hand to the floor and heaves his bulk onto his feet.

He bends to return the drawer to its place.

He looks upon her, this beautiful creature.

He turns and ducks under and out of the little door.

She can hear him outside. The clump of a heavy bag hitting the earth and the rasping of curved shell on shell. She opens her eyes, raises herself to her elbows and looks down her body. This thing he has put on her she does not know. She smooths her hands down it. And then she rises, steps from the mat and, wobbling, she heads towards the door.

Outside, Uncle Mike has spread a length of green netting across the patch of sand. On this he has poured three of his five bags of clam. He adds the fourth, a clattering shower of shell, and then the fifth. The shells are still cold from the ocean. From where she stands in the little doorway, she can smell them.

Despite herself she looks up to the drying cephalopod. Its head has sunken further and its tentacles have begun to wither.

Uncle Mike catches her glance.

He steps to the work table where a knife lies. He grasps it and reaches up to pull a severed tentacle from the eaves above. The serpentine arm thumps down, its suckers rigid in their rows.

He slices a wedge from the arm and holds it up to her.

She shakes her head. '*No.*'

Uncle Mike shrugs and returns to his work. He takes up a clam in his fist. In the other he holds his knife, which he slips into the lips of the shell to sever the muscle. He pries the shell open and with his fingers he probes the flesh within. He withdraws his hand, holding a pearl between thumb and forefinger. He raises it to his eye. It is perfect.

She regards him, her pearl in his fingers, the broken shell of her clam, and the shadow of the cephalopod covering them both. She imprints his vast shape within her. She nods to him once, and then releases her feet to their bidding. She moves past him, and clicks through the gate, and beneath her bare feet the small plants crunch softly as she makes her way round the side of the hut through the low bushes of the veld, heading for the mountains.

'You will need water,' he calls to her.

She stops at the sound of his words. He knows she understands.

She stands for moment, motionless in the golden evening. And then finally, she walks on. Uncle Mike drops his eyes. He sits quiet, keenly aware of her going, until he raises his eyes once again. He finds her in the vastness out there, the white of her dress merging with the coming twilight. Above her the mountains loom.

He says nothing, does nothing, simply allowing all that she is to pass through him.

'How can she be?' he mutters, before turning to his harvest once again. He drops his new pearl into the bucket of fresh water placed beside him, and then reaches for the next clam. He takes up his knife.

Uncle Mike continues working into the night. He fetches lights salvaged from Mocke's *fabriek*. He yanks a little red generator into clattering life, and by its charge the patch of sand is lit up. The clams lie in a mottled pile, now dry.

Uncle Mike stops suddenly, and stares. Dry.

'Stupid,' he rumbles to himself.

Ten of the clams he has opened and in each he has found a perfect pearl, exactly the dimension of the pearl he still has in his pocket. Ten of the clams is enough to confirm that they are blessed and fertile, and ten is enough for him to raise the finances he needs. But dry clams will not help him. He needs them alive.

'Stupid,' he rumbles once more as he lumbers to the rear of the hut. In his fist he carries a penlight torch and he uses the handle to knock the lid off of the first water tank. He dips his finger into the water and tastes it. Salt. He nods and then easily hefts the whole tank from its base, leaving a damp world of beetle and worm woken to the night sky. He raises the tank to his shoulder and returns to his clams. Quickly he drops them in.

'I will put some new water in tomorrow,' he murmurs to himself as the last of the black shells sink to the bottom. He has cleared the netting at his feet, and the mess of the already opened clams is littered around him. He scoops up the pieces of meat and flings them over the fence into the darkened veld. The smell of the sea covers everything.

'Let the seagulls eat,' he mutters, scraping all the muck off of the netting that he can, and then wiping his fingers off on the fence. 'Something can eat, at least.'

It is then, when he is ready to clean and repair his new gear that he hears the beat of an engine. He looks out into the darkness.

'It must be Mocke, or maybe Van Deventer. Yoguchi is looking for the boy, so they are looking for him also.'

He sees a glow of lights out on the tar road. He narrows his eyes. They are searching for the boy without consulting with him first. That means betrayal.

The smell of money has them coming forward, he knows. He turns to his spread of equipment. Quickly he begins to stow it away. An armful he hauls to his motor and drops into the flatbed before spreading a chipped blue tarp over the clutter, and the rest he packs near the worktable as if it is the boy's own. The water tank catches his eye.

'Stupid,' he mutters as the lights of the approaching motor sweep the sand just up the way. He places the lid on top and knocks it in place, just as the light wipes across the hut and dazzles his eyes. He shields his face with his hand.

He cannot see the motor, but he can sense that it is not one that he knows. Mocke would be driving his little Datsun, Van Deventer would be in his big Toyota *bakkie* – his white pickup. This motor is neither. This motor purrs, and its outline is long and low.

A silhouette appears behind the light, standing up out of the driver door and walking round to the rear of the vehicle. There it bends and a door clicks, and a new silhouette steps out. Uncle Mike screws his eyes trying to see.

'Turn down your brights! You can see I am standing here.'

The lights extinguish, and at the same time the motor cuts. Now it is the work lights that pierce the night, and Mr Yoguchi steps into their glare.

'Mr Morkel.'

'Mr Yoguchi.'

'Is the young fisherman at home?'

'He has gone to sea, up the coast I believe. He left two days ago.' Uncle Mike eyes the driver sitting idle. This motor must have come from the town an hour's drive away; he has not seen it in the Baai before.

'You like my motorcar? I brought it with me. I have found it good to come prepared when visiting another land. It's better to ask nothing, and to give much. People are suspicious.' Yoguchi makes a show of eyeing out the hut. Uncle Mike resists the urge to block his view of the tank standing in the open.

'Us outsiders must work a little harder, to get what we want.'

'Why are you looking for the boy?'

'He is an exceptional talent. Who knows, maybe he can show us how he found that beautiful blue sailfish?' Yoguchi fishes a package of cigarettes from his jacket pocket, and with a rasp of flint on wheel he lights it. 'What is your relationship to the boy, if I may ask?'

'He works for me.'

Yoguchi nods, drawing the smoke deep while looking about him at the dark veld, and further to the darker mountains. 'I have heard. I am told also that you are not the most patient of employers.'

'People talk all sorts of nonsense.'

'You are not from here. You are from the mountains?' Yoguchi gestures out to the dark. 'I come from across the ocean. Very, very far, and I am more at home here than yourself.' He runs the fingers of his left hand lightly along the drooping wire of the boy's fence. 'I could see it that day we went fishing along with your friends. You are like a bear, on a boat.'

'And you are like a snake. No ship anywhere in the world enjoys a snake on board.'

Yoguchi laughs. He wipes his palm across his forehead.

'Snakes keep the vermin down, they are useful.' He drags deep, for a moment the coal of his cigarette glows in his eyes. 'The boy had an injured shoulder that day. He hid it well. But I could tell he was in pain. It is you that caused him the injury.'

'If I did it's between me and the boy.'

'Your anger must be something!' Yoguchi puts his hand out to measure against the meat of Uncle Mike's own palm: a spoon to a spade. 'What are you doing here tonight? You are trying with the boy to discover how we refrigerate?'

Uncle Mike blinks. All these things this man would have known, but not the refrigeration. Surely that was a secret for the men of the Baai.

Yoguchi looks at him sideways. 'You underestimate your place here, as a man of the Baai. You are not one of them, and you never will be. You are the outsider.' Yoguchi looks away to the dark veld, at the same time he crushes his cigarette to the fence post. Sparks fall to the sand. 'The nights here are cool, and fresh. In my homeland the air is frozen.'

'The boy is not here. There is nothing here for you.'

'Come now, bear man. Let us not waste this precious time we have been given, you and I. Every man gets his chance, not so? Tonight you have been given one. A chance meeting with the only man in this little town that can help you.' Yoguchi shuffles his sneakers in the sand, observing the fine dust that rises. 'Do you know the country from which I come? It is a place that would devastate you, my big friend. The harbour of my home would make your eyes pop; it would make you crawl into a hole when you think of your little refrigeration project. You have no inkling of our power, but you can surely feel it. You know, my bear friend, that you *do not know*.'

Uncle Mike moves then, a flicker in the darkness, and suddenly the chin of Yoguchi is cradled in his hand. Yoguchi is shocked, his eyes wide. Behind, the driver stumbles up and out of the motor, full of fright.

'Well!' breathes Yoguchi.

Uncle Mike regards him quietly. His eyes shift to the driver who now has a pistol in his hand. 'You are right, I am not a man of the sea. I am not a dirty fisherman, like yourself, living your life in the muck of slimy beings. I am a man who knows war.'

Uncle Mike increases the pressure around the bone of Yoguchi's chin. The little man's eyes bulge. 'It seems there are things in this world that cause your eyes to pop also, my little friend.' Lightly, Uncle Mike releases his face.

Yoguchi's eyes shine with excitement. He reaches up to massage his jaw. '*Rirakkusu*,' he murmurs to the agitated driver, 'put it down.'

'As you say, every man gets his chance. Tell me, what is the chance you are offering me?'

'I came here looking for a child, and instead I found a giant. Just as the boy is an anomaly, so are you. Join me, before your so-called brothers sell you out.'

'And what would you offer me?'

'A future. A way for you to survive what is coming.'

'And what is coming?'

'The end of the world,' says Yoguchi, watching him as a snake watches, from a black, unblinking eye. 'And a new world after that, one in which only the lucky, and the protected, will thrive.'

The black eye of the snake watches the black eye of the bear.

'You know much, little man. But you have made an error.'

'What error have I made?'

'You have assumed that I am like you. You have assumed that the world is like you. You think that I want what you want.'

'What do you want?'

'I want you gone. I want your ships wrecked on this beach. I want you and your thieving kind wiped from the earth.' Uncle Mike smiles. 'Now, slither back to the tunnel you call your home.'

Yoguchi leans back, his neck extending in a sinuous line as he looks up to the stars.

'Ah! Look: *Yo watashi boshi*.' He points to the three stars that form the belt of Orion. 'The belt of the warrior, the one who would hunt all the creatures of the world.' He takes a step back. 'We have few stories of the stars. For us, the story of the hunter who would defy the gods is nothing at all, merely a woman pointing at no one, with the sleeve of her kimono hanging down.'

Yoguchi touches his finger to his temple, a mock salute.

'Mr Morkel. It is a privilege for me to meet you. I am sure we will meet again soon.'

Uncle Mike watches as the little man returns to his motor, and as it retreats down the sandy track. He hunches his shoulders as solitude returns. He looks back to his clams, undiscovered in their tank: the future of his Baai. In the cool night he feels the storm that is coming, and he knows what he must do.

CHAPTER TEN

The summer winds have come to the Baai, and they are violent this afternoon. Uncle Mike is sitting in his motor, readying himself to meet with the six. He looks out past the buildings of Van Deventer's *fabriek* to the ocean that froths beneath the driving gale. Yoguchi's words swirl through him, just as the wind swirls on the water. They have been harrying him all night. 'You are not one of them, and you never will be. You are the outsider.'

The little man is right of course. Uncle Mike knows it and has always known it. Despite having been a man of the Baai for twenty years, and even though he worked his way from a *handlanger* – a labourer – to the owner of his own *fabriek*, carving a place for himself among the seven, and even though he has never once given any of them reason to mistrust him, or even given less than his all for the good of the Baai, still he is not one of them. It has been a long while since he has felt it so keenly. But so it is. When fear rises, so the truth of men's allegiances are revealed. These men will look to each other first, despite Mocke's assertion that only the old *strandlopers* are the true residents of this place.

There is the rumble of a motor, and Uncle Mike looks up to see the Toyota of Weatherall-Thomas gliding past. The man behind the wheel is obscured by the passenger door, so high is the double-cabbed truck to Uncle Mike's Datsun. In the passenger seat he sees young Cryno, Weatherall-Thomas's first-born. Uncle Mike knows the boy from the harbour, in the early mornings when the *snoek* fish are running and the place is swarming with light craft, and the fishermen and their boys are gathered in their squeaking oilskins. He knows the boy by the orange of the harbour floodlights strung high above the concrete, his strawberry hair still tousled from his bed, where he'd lain not thirty minutes before, his young fingers holding a cigarette, already calloused and scarred from the lines. '*Goeie môre, Oom. Hoe gaan dit met Oom?* – Good morning, Uncle. How is Uncle?' he has often heard him say, offering his strong back to carry the nets. But there is none of that now; the uncertainty of the times has taken friendship from his eyes. Uncle Mike looks ahead to the others clustered near the double doors of Van Deventer's sorting hall. Strategy. He can see it in every look and gesture. They have closed ranks, and the last one in, the seventh, is here to earn his place or leave.

Uncle Mike sighs. He is aware of the flow of time. He is aware of the day he arrived in this Baai with nothing but a hessian sack of the small things he and his wife scavenged on their way from the mountains. He remembers the first sight of the town on the long curve of the bay, and her hand in his as together they walked down.

He sighs once more, and clicks open the door of the Datsun. The wind covers the creaking of the little car as he leaves it. He walks towards them. They are harried, the wind plucks at them also, and their eyes are on him. Their faces pinch as he nears; a shadow passes over them all.

'Chisto,' says Uncle Mike, extending his paw to Van Deventer. The man's life at sea has given him hands of iron, and as usual he grips with all his strength. Just this once, today, Uncle Mike returns the squeeze.

'Mikey,' grunts Van Deventer, pulling his hand away.

'Thys,' says Uncle Mike to old Mocke, the next in line, who extends a thoughtful hand. There is no malice in the old man's touch. He too remembers the day the giant from the mountains arrived with the woman at his side. He remembers how the young man worked unceasingly, taking on any task after the woman had died. He remembers him lumbering daily the long sand road to the Meintjies *fabriek* from the hut he built from scraps, and he recalls whispering a word of endorsement in the ear of Trevor Meintjies, the man whose *fabriek* Mikey was destined to inherit once he passed away.

'How the days fade,' thinks old Mocke as he looks into the eyes of the big man, and wishes him well with a gentle squeeze.

'*Manne* – men.' Uncle Mike gestures to the others, who one by one extend their hands. In each touch is a memory, for the good years and bad years run deep between them all.

'How goes it, Mike?' asks Van Deventer, by way of pulling the meeting to order.

'*Redelik* – well,' responds Mike, looking to a trio of gulls huddled on the two-way aerial of the *Van Deventer 2* rolling at rope nearby. 'And with you?'

'*Ja, ja*,' nods Van Deventer, casting his eyes about the group.

'Shall we go inside?' murmurs Mocke.

'*Ja*, we can,' gruffs Van Deventer.

'But where is your boy?' Weatherall-Thomas asks this, his two index fingers hooked into the loops of his denims and his eyes looking up to Uncle Mike. 'You said you would bring him.'

Uncle Mike shrugs his big shoulders. 'I cannot find him. I think he has gone fishing, up north.'

Van Deventer and Weatherall-Thomas share a look.

'How long has he been gone for, Mikey?' asks Mocke quietly.

'I don't know. The last I saw him was two days ago. He does this sometimes. He is a strange one.'

'Agh! What did I say?' This is Nico Schaafsma speaking, now reaching for a Camel from his pack.

'Okay, Nico,' says Mocke, laying a finger on the younger man's arm.

Uncle Mike allows his eyes to sweep over the six, finally coming to rest on those of young Cryno, who quickly looks away.

'Is there a problem, with the boy not being here?'

'Mikey, we asked you to bring the boy. We have business to talk with him.' The tone of Van Deventer's voice forces the others into silence. 'That was the purpose of our meeting.'

'The last I recall the boy is not one of us. He is my *handlanger*, to bring as I please.'

'Ever since your boy took us straight to a blue sailfish with no echo finder, I think we all have an interest in him.' Weatherall-Thomas eyes Uncle Mike. His fingers are still looped beside his belt, but now his chin has risen.

'Mikey, the boy could be very important for us. Yoguchi has told us he would like to meet him.'

'You have been speaking to him without me?'

'Ugh!' hisses Weatherall-Thomas, shooting a glance to Nico, who shakes his head and looks away to the gulls.

'The boy's boat is still on the beach, and his nets. They are dry.' Mark Schaafsma says this quietly but clearly, his eyes fixed to Uncle Mike's broad chest. Now he looks up. '*Oom* Mike, we know he's not fishing.'

'That boy is not my concern. If you want him, why don't you find him?'

'Mikey,' says Van Deventer, taking the big man by his elbow and walking with him away from the group. 'We are all on the same side...'

Uncle Mike moves his arm away and turns back to the six. 'What has Yoguchi said? I have not heard anything of him. What were his words? What does he say about our offer?'

'He says very little,' answers Mocke carefully. 'He thanked us for it, and said that he is sure there will be time for us to work together on a piecemeal basis. He has told us he would value friendship, and skill exchanges, as he does not know our sea. He wants our permission to dock in our harbour, and to fish our deep waters where we cannot go. He says he will pay us good berthing fees, and he offers us the part of his future catch that he cannot process himself. Further than that, he hopes a man of the Baai who could advise his ships on the best practice for catching in our waters can be provided. To this end he mentioned your boy.'

'He also mentions that in the future, as his crew rotate out, he sees the opportunity to place some of our young fishers on his ships,' adds Weatherall-Thomas. 'What do you say to that?'

Weatherall-Thomas is glaring at Uncle Mike, his chin with his silver dusting of beard thrust far out from his chest. His hands are now fists around his belt. Next to him, Cryno stands, unable to glare at Uncle Mike, but undoubtedly supporting his father. They are mirrors of each other. Both red-haired, with blue eyes shining from their ruddy faces, Cryno's beard a shadow of his father's.

And then Uncle Mike knows why they have summoned him, and why they have not gone inside. Why he has never been one of them, and never will be. These are men of the sea. They know the possibility of not returning when they set out, but they also long to return. These are family men, with loved ones who wait and watch when they are away on the blue, and who line the quay when they return, and cheer not for the holds full of frozen fish but rather for the light in the eyes of their loves as they step onto dry land, still safe. These are men that fight to preserve their children; their children are their peace and their homes their honour. Uncle Mike is alone. He casts a shadow over their hearths with his solitude. He wishes it were not so, but it is. They do not trust him because there is no other that holds him accountable on this earth. Now is the time to secure their homes, they think, even if the act condemns them forever.

'You wish to sell our Baai,' says Uncle Mike.

'Oh, for fuck's sake!' Nico Schaafsma kicks the ground.

'That is what you suggest; that is what you want me to agree to.'

'Mikey, this is an opportunity for us,' yells Weatherall-Thomas suddenly, spit spraying from his mouth, Mark Schaafsma grabbing an arm to hold him back. 'This is our chance to get out of this fucking mess! There are no fish!'

'You believe Yoguchi in this talk of togetherness? You think he will preserve our Baai? You think he will not take what he needs and then be off, with our ocean truly empty? You think you are something but pawns in his game?'

'What do we do then, Mikey?'

Uncle Mike turns to the watery eyes of Mocke. They recognise all that is being said here, that know the process of fear and its outcomes.

'Why can't we try another way? Why can't we farm? You did it. Why can't we try it?'

'Mikey...' The old man spreads his hands. 'We are fishermen. We don't have the ability to do that. I have tried. I could not make it work.'

Uncle Mike opens his mouth to argue, but something stops him. He can see it. They know he will never agree; they have made their decision.

'Tell us where the boy is, Mikey. It will help us with our talks with Yoguchi. We want the best for our people.'

Uncle Mike turns to the speaker, Van Deventer.

'Yoguchi has offered us an even split, seven ways, for the harvest he brings in. We will buy your share, Mikey. We will give you a good price.'

'We are not like you; we are not fighters like you.' Weatherall-Thomas's chin has sunk to his chest. 'We have families, Mikey.'

Uncle Mike lets his eyes pass over each of them, every face he has known for these twenty years. Friends once.

'I understand,' he rumbles. 'You are looking to make the best of it. But, once you let him in, it is over. He will eat our Baai and spit out our bones. Soon, all that will be left of us will be skeletons littered across the beach.'

He puts out his hand. He touches the palm of each man in turn.

'As for paying me for my share, please don't worry. Look after my workers. That's all I ask.'

Uncle Mike turns his eyes to old Mocke. The one he will miss most. He finds the old man watching him flatly. Suddenly he smiles, a smile in honour of all the years and it is a splendid thing. Uncle Mike finds it easy and true and he smiles at him in turn. And then he offers his hand to all of them again, touching their fingers one by one.

'Keep your money for the years ahead,' he rumbles, as he turns to trudge back to his motor.

'I don't know where the boy is,' he calls to them as he walks, half turning to see them one last time: a group of men cast together, the wind pulling at them. 'He ran north from me three days ago. I suspect you will not see him again.'

'You were never one of us, Mikey,' calls Van Deventer. 'We are simple folk. We want to eat our fish, that is all. You and we are not the same.'

He walks from them, leaving the six and their ways behind.

Uncle Mike drives angrily. He had hoped for support in his plan; he was wishing for an agreement to resist Yoguchi.

'I hope they drown,' he mutters, and then he remembers the fear in all of their eyes. He sighs. 'I hope they find their peace,' he amends, as he clicks his indicator to turn into the forecourt of the petrol station. His stomach is rumbling; it has been a full day since he last ate. He will get fish and chips at the shop, and Coca-Cola, and then he will head back to the hut. His thoughts turn to the creature as he walks the empty forecourt and the brightly lit red-and-white sign: Jovanti's Video & Take-Aways, ahead of him.

'Where is she now?' he wonders as he enters the plastic and vegetable jumble of the little shop. He passes Julia, the daughter of Alex Jovanti, sitting behind the till, her face turned to the flickering TV. 'She will come back,' he mutters. 'If she does not find him, she will be back. And if she does, let her be.'

'*Naand*, Alex – good evening,' says Uncle Mike as he reaches the take-away counter in the back of the shop. Behind it, Alex Jovanti stands in his habitual pose – round chin above round shoulders, hands clasped over his round belly, eyes trained on the door. 'A double hake and chips.' Uncle Mike slides a tattered note onto the counter. 'And a two-litre Coke please, Alex.'

'*Naand*, Uncle Mike,' nods Alex, turning to set to the order. 'Will you have some coleslaw?'

Uncle Mike looks at the display of limp salads beneath the counter. He likes a coleslaw, the mayo always goes well with the salt of the chips and the fish, but he is hungry tonight. 'I'll take a pasta salad, *asseblief* – please – Alex.'

The shopkeeper nods as he goes about dishing battered fish wedges into a polystyrene take-away container, dropping a rain of sizzling chips into another. He starts to season the pile with a dusting of red chip spice and glugs of vinegar. The man moves little, and speaks little, and has been in the Baai for as long Uncle Mike himself. He had the first petrol pump in the town outside of the harbour, and rumour says he got a good price to sell his plot to Caltex. Now he deals his take-aways like he always did, but with a wedge of cash under his mattress. Uncle Mike smiles. Like him, Alex Jovanti is an outsider. Twenty years long he has lived on Bovertrek Street with his wife and three daughters who, one by one, started working in his shop and who then, one by one, went away to marry boys from the Baai.

'Have you seen the paper?'

'Why?'

'That ship of the foreigners is in there.' Jovanti nods to the shop paper on the counter, smeared with oily fingerprints. With one hand Uncle Mike folds it open.

The front page stops him cold. On it there is an artist's impression of a ship.

'They want to bring it to our harbour,' says Alex, now wrapping Uncle Mike's three parcels in clingfilm. 'It says it's ten storeys. Ten storeys!' Alex Jovanti shakes his head in disbelief.

Uncle Mike touches his finger to the picture. It is flat and lifeless. Beneath it is the caption: *Full schematic on page 5!*

Uncle Mike takes up the paper and flips through it.

'Mikey?'

Uncle Mike looks up to Alex holding out his steaming parcels. He does not reach to take them. He does not want to drop the paper.

'You want to take that paper? It's the end of the day.'

'*Dankie*, Alex – thank you.'

He tucks the paper under his arm and takes up the three parcels. He begins to walk toward the door.

'Uncle Mike!'

He turns.

'Your Coke.'

Alex is pointing at the cooldrink fridges next to the racks of DVDs.

'*Ja*. Thanks.'

With his left hand he swings the door open, reaches in and hooks a two-litre bottle.

'Thanks again,' he calls as he passes Julia at the till.

In his motor, Uncle Mike puts his parcels on the passenger seat, spreads the paper on his lap, and twists the lid off the bottle. He does not drink long. Instead, he turns his attention to the paper. The world pauses in its turning. Here before him rises the greatest ship he could ever imagine. Intricate diagrams trace across the double spread in the middle of the paper, forming a floating city that he simply cannot comprehend. Parts of it are familiar: in it he sees the logic of his own factory, the necessity of the processes that are his bread and butter, but together they describe a reality far beyond what he can fathom. A sensation rises in his gut: dread. He marks it. For the first time in many years, he is afraid.

You have no idea of the power standing before you... Yoguchi's words from the night before sigh through his brain. *Your eyes would pop if you saw what I have seen...*

Uncle Mike turns his chin from side to side, feeling the new world that this ship brings, this horrifying world. He sits thus, the howling future cradled in his lap.

'They were right.'

He closes his eyes and sees Yoguchi's face swelling to the pressure of his fingers; he sees the fear in his eyes.

'You are human, just like all of us,' he whispers as he traces the lines of the machine on the pages. 'You are blood and bone.'

Uncle Mike reaches his hand up to turn the key in the ignition. The forecourt of the empty petrol station revolves behind him and the nearby mountains fill the windscreen as he reverses, pointing the motor's bonnet to the road.

He turns into it, speeding towards the hut.

At the same time as Uncle Mike is turning his little Datsun west on the old coast road, so up on the mountain, raised above all of the little village of the Baai, she sits. She is at the place Jono brought her to. Before her the coast stretches away to the north, drawing its jagged white line to the horizon. To the west, the land falls away to dusk. The world is vast and empty.

She reaches out to touch the legs stretched before her. They have swollen. The skin is blotched red, blue and white and stretched taut. In places, behind the knee, at the ankle and between the toes, it has split. She has learned quickly that even though she has left the sea, her flesh needs water. And her legs, unused to walking, are full of the torture of the hike to this place.

Every step of her journey upward she had hoped to find his sign. Evidence of his cart cut into the earth, or his footprints, or a place of a burned-out cooking fire. But she cannot understand this waterless world. In the ocean she could discern the origin of any current and drift with it for days, but here no secrets are revealed. The soil remains a mystery, the waving of the flower carpet beneath the wind and that same wind on her skin is unknown to her. And the rocks beneath her feet. They are the worst. She looks at her soles. They are ripped up. Over and over she has pierced them on the jagged trail, and scraped them, and ground them. She crawled the final stretch up here, sure of the path, sure of her memory, and now, finally, she is at the place that he would find her, or her him, if it is to be. And he is not here.

The world howls at her as the wind rages. Out there, the sea has turned to striated froth. Behind her the hills shiver beneath the wind's assault.

'*I would even eat some rabbit tonight.*' She leans back so that her head rests on the wall of sandstone behind her. '*I will watch the sunset, and it will be beautiful.*'

As she looks at the sun, her mind travels back. She remembers his body flickering in that light. All the fine muscle of him, and the scarring, and the grace. She feels all the promise in him, all of the mystery of him, all of her future with him, waiting for her. She longs for him. It is in her stomach, a hole inside her through which her life is leaking. She puts her arms over it, cradling herself.

'*There is a whole world out there,*' he had said to her, his dancing brown eyes looking into her own. '*There are cities out there, places where schools of people live.*'

She remembers his body climbing into the tank with her; she feels it, his flesh alive against her own. He is an animal she does not know; he is a force she does not know. His arms curling around her, his heart beating beside her own. He is the world beyond, and without him, the world is dead. The wind howls on the mountaintop, and it howls through the emptiness within her.

'*Where is the hunter in the sky now?*' she wonders, looking up to the winking of the first stars. '*If he is real, if he is there, let him take me. Let the scorpion take me. Let all the emptiness take me.*'

She closes her eyes and finds her memories. She sees a shadow circling lazily above and hears the plop of hook and sinker as the line falls through the veil, and she marvels at the fish taken up and away. She waits eagerly, for she knows that soon she will be taken up, like one of those fishes, and she will once again look into his eyes. As the wind howls through the dark night, and the hunter and scorpion beam down on her, she smiles in her painful sleep, and whispers his name to the moon.

In the morning she is stiff and sore. The sun has risen and it is bright in her tired eyes. The night wind is gone. In the tranquility of morning she sees the tiny town gathered at the water, and the awesome sea. A black *korhaan* calls to his mate from the bush nearby. She watches it pecking in the tufted grass, its cackling turning through the air.

'*I will stay here,*' she thinks to herself, feeling the numbness of her legs and back. '*I have gone as far as I know how.*'

Her eyes move to the magnificent blue at rest.

The world is spread before her. There is nothing she can do to change it.

She is about to lie back when something on the plain catches her eye. There, struggling along the sandy track that she knows, is a man pulling a cart.

She sits up. Her heart is beating hard in her chest. She fights the ache in her body and struggles to her feet, scaring the *korhaan*. She limps to the rock wall beside her to look. Yes. A man is moving upon the road down there, and behind him he pulls a load that rises above his head. It is her love; she is sure of it. She begins to hobble her way down the path.

'*I'm coming*,' she pants, ignoring the pain in her shattered legs, '*I'm coming!*'

But she cannot go far. Her new legs soon give way and she sinks to her knees. She crawls through the sand and the rocks, but even her crawling slows, and finally she is only inching her way down the path in the deep shadow of the sandstone that rises on either side of her. She stops. It is pointless.

'*I hope he will come this way.*'

It is near noon when she hears the creaking of the cart approaching. Her throat is desiccated and her eyes have dimmed. She looks up to see a massive silhouette grinding up the path to meet her. It has the legs of a man, larger than a man, but its body is round and rises up huge, blocking out the sun.

'*My love?*' she sounds in her mind, but there is no answer.

The silhouette grinds to a halt before her.

'*Jonothan?*'

The creature looms over her. Fear sounds. It is not human. Somehow, she has crossed over. It is a monster that has found her up here on this alien plain. It is the hunter himself, Orion, come to take her from Gaia. '*I should never have left my home*,' she thinks, as the monster reaches down. She feels strong hands collecting her. They raise her up and lay her across a back as hard and broad as the mountain.

'*Orion has come to take me*,' she thinks, and thinks no more.

CHAPTER ELEVEN

The monster grinds along a winding mountain trail. Its body is long and creaks through the many twists and rocky turns. It is constructed of wood and flesh, and it locomotes on leg and wheel. At its end is the backside of a creaking cart festooned with the creatures of the sea. Nymphs swim through the whorls of its wood, and seahorses, and spiralling whales. Hammered into the wood are clamps and latches onto which are secured pipes and pipettes, pumps and vials, and coils of marine tubing. Above the cart, rising ten feet into the air, is a swaying load. It is held by a giant swathe of blue tarpaulin, secured by rope netting and ratchet strap, and inside it are the leavings of the old abalone farm of Mocke Fisheries Inc. Pump and sealant, and filtration system and lumber, and reef mix and hydrometer, and woodworking equipment – saw and nail and hammer and measure.

While the abdomen that rises high is constructed of cart and rubber and metal, the head of the monster is flesh and bone. A bear of a man is strapped into the contraption, and step by step he drags it across the peak. His eyes are dark and focused not on the mountain turning before him, but rather on the past. The trail is an artery running toward the history of his own heart. Each turning is known to him.

He has made use of it three times. The first was when he travelled to the Baai as a young man, where his new life began, and then twice more he used this road to mark the passing of the dead.

It is their memory that drives him, and so he follows a wild plan. Behind him, deep in the centre of the wooden cart that he discovered under tarp at Jono's beach, is a sealed tank in which oxygen pumps and ocean water sloshes. Within that bubbling water lie the dark shapes of bivalves, their shells ajar and their whiskers examining the gloom. There are twelve of them, clams that he has already harvested, their pearls buried safely in the veld behind the boy's hut, clams ready to be impregnated and to grow their fine pearls again.

They are fragile. Without antibiotics and proper filtration they will die, and all of his plans with them. They are like lungs breathing, lending oxygen to his dreams, and so he knows he must push hard day and night.

As he toils in a world of pain, one sensation brings sweetness.

As light as gossamer she is laid across his shoulders. She is dead to the world, moaning fitfully as the rocky track jars her through his shoulders. It is she that reminds him to tread carefully, to not abandon himself to exhaustion; her moans that bring him back to the world when exhaustion attempts to pull him away.

He rests when his body demands it, simply grinding to a halt and with relief reaching up to unclasp the hitch of the yoke at his sternum, taking pleasure in sinking to the unforgiving rock and taking nourishment from the solidity of the mountain.

His means of unloading her are always the same. He leans down so that his forehead nearly touches the rock and scoops his hand up behind his neck. Then he gently wipes her from his shoulder and lets her slide across his back and arm to the earth. He cradles her head before it touches rock, and places a burlap sack beneath it.

Sometimes during their rest she lies dead and unseeing, and other times, precisely which he has forgotten within the merging of this relentless walk, her eyes flutter open and once again he peers into those green pools.

At times he finds himself staring at a wall of rock himself, and realises he was out of the world, dead on his feet. But mostly he tends to her. Her legs have swollen even further, becoming grotesque worms. Water splashed from the tank does wonders on her skin, but he cannot risk the health of his clams and so he turns to the seal lard stored in an old paint tin at the side of the cart. As they rest in the middle of the road with the load of the cart rising over them, he rubs the lard into her, whether it is by day with the sun beaming down, or by night when the stars wheel and leopards stalk the dark.

As the journey progresses so he feels the creature sinking deeper.

'You were not built for this place,' he rumbles as he trudges. 'You were built for the cold and the deep. You should have stayed there.' But despite his sentiment he squeezes her calf, wanting her to feel comfort. 'Stay with me. Soon, I will bring you water. Our place is beautiful, you will see. It will heal you.'

And he looks ahead once again, and permits himself to smile in his solitude. For he was born on the mountain, the rock brings him comfort, and he is going home.

It is late afternoon on the third day when he knows that they are close. He remembers this turn in the track well. It is an alcove where a little olive tree grows, positioned beside the track, seeming to spring from the bare rock as a perfect miniature, but with no discernible soil from which it grows. He remembers studying this fantastic creature for the first time, twenty years ago, marvelling at its ability to burrow through rock. He remembers discovering its secret. He goes nearer, and once again finds the hidden overhang. He sees the little pool of soil there, into which the roots of the tree have twisted. Once again he traces them as they climb through the air to form the hardy tree above.

'You are truly magic,' he says to the little plant. 'I am so glad to see you again.'

Half an hour later Uncle Mike finally stops, placing one hand against the sheer cliff beside him while with the other he steadies the creature on his shoulder. Here it lies, a little lake, nestled in the rising buttresses of the mountain. Here it lies, this place that is his heart.

The trail ahead peels off and down to meet the water's edge. There the pool lies deep and cold, its edges ruffled by a waterfall on the far side that tumbles from the cliff-face above. From where he stands the trail tracks round to the left, rising to the same cliff. To his right and to the west, after the waterfall, the cliff gives way to a pocket of *karee* and ash trees, an unexpected forest this high up that rings that portion of the pool.

His eyes linger on the trees. If this hidden lake in the mountains is a home, the trees are its heart. He breathes deep, and then with an effort he turns his eyes away. The trees will be his reward. First, there is work to be done.

He unhitches the yoke and gently slides the creature from his shoulder. With her in his arms he tramps down to the water's edge, careful over bare rock coated with the waterfall's mist. He kneels to lay her at the edge and then he goes down to his knees beside her. He kisses the rock.

'*Thank you.*'

He stands. He removes his clothes and feels once again what it is to be free in the mountain. The waterfall rushes, and doves and weavers call.

He takes up the creature and steps into the water. It climbs to his waist and higher, where now it touches her body also. She shivers like a fish. He continues, letting the water rise till it covers him all the way to his shoulders and she floats seven feet above the grim rock below.

He stands quietly, drinking every detail. The cliffs rise bare and full of ledges. There is bashful life up there: rock rabbits shelter in cracks and frogs peer from the pool. The peace of the place flows into him. This water, this precious water.

Again a shiver runs through her body. He waits.

Suddenly, she kicks away from him.

He watches.

She is not yet awake, but he can see that in some way she is aware.

And then she opens her green eyes.

She sees blue sky and around it a ring of rock pierced by a waterfall. She drifts, and then there is the feel of flesh against her ankle.

His hand.

She turns to see his face. His dark hair is plastered to his forehead, and his dark beard and moustache gleam with water.

She flicks herself away, circling out into the lake, little twists of her hands taking her further. As the water washes her so slices of memory return – pain as she rode upon his shoulders, his bone and muscle digging into her, and pain as she lay on the rock, and fever.

She looks around at the trees and the sheer rock and the wide calm of the water. She licks her tongue across her upper lip. The water is sweet.

He is watching her. She cannot read his expression and she wants nothing to do with his thoughts. She wants to pulse her fin and dive, but her legs trail beneath her, useless.

Like a bear he begins to swim, his arms and legs paddling below and only his face above. She gives him a wide berth.

He stops in the centre of the lake, treading water. He casts his eyes up to the cliff, staring for a moment, and then he dives, and disappears. She looks to the cliff. She sees nothing but rock rearing above her; she does not like this place of heights.

She peers through the surface of the water, looking for him below. Down there it is dark, the shade from the cliff making the water black. She takes a breath, still unused to the need to fill her lungs, and tips herself over.

Underneath she finds rocky walls sloping down. Here, weed grows from deeper soil. Some luminous and some pale, they drift in the murmuring sunlight. Between them fly new kinds of fish. A long grey creature with black eyes traverses the weeds, biting at the stalks, and another, mottled green and brown. This one bulges behind the head, a fat torso tapering back to a slender tail with fins frilled like an eel. It passes her, its body snaking through the water.

She drifts half way down, flying once again, free once again. A white boulder rears from the weed below. She senses movement. Below the boulder something is rising, and then he appears. He climbs up to her, one hand scooping water while the other is a fist punching ahead, a smile splitting the granite of his face. She turns to watch as his huge form breaks the surface.

Bubbles explode around him and light refracts. Here below there is peace for her, but soon she feels a burning in her chest and limbs. She examines it, this pain, and then her lungs begin to pump against her closed gills. The sensation drives her to the dancing silver up there, and she breaks clear.

She floats with her face to the sky, breathing in the mist of the waterfall. She turns her face from the spray and there he is, treading water.

He extends his hand to her and opens his fingers. There are two brown freshwater clams in his palm, only a third of the size of those from her cave. He presses the little creatures into her fingers, and then turns and strikes out to the shore.

In the hot sun Uncle Mike sets to work. Ever since he hatched this plan four days before, he has been preparing for this moment of arrival. His first goal is to separate the cart from the load as easily as possible. First, he unclips the ratchet strap that bisects the bulging blue tarpaulin. He pulls the strap away so that it hisses to the ground, leaving the previously taut tarp to sag to the pressure of the equipment within. Next, he turns to the several clamps that he has sunk into the wood of the cart. He releases them, freeing the netting that he has criss-crossed over the load. The bulge above begins to lean towards him.

Uncle Mike allows it to slide onto his chest. He grunts, taking a step backwards, swaying with it. His face grows red as he shifts the weight sideways, angling for the cliff wall beside him. There he wedges the load against the rock, and assisted by the friction of the wall he bends until he is seated on the ground. Here in this sliver of shade the aroma is of moist earth, and distant sun, and mossy rock. He shifts the tower sideways, allowing it to slide onto the earth also. His hands are smeared with soil.

With the load removed he returns to the cart. His solar panel is still attached to the yoke and he retrieves it, examining the fine connecting wires. They are unbroken, the panel seems undamaged, and the whir of the little Jebao pump inside the sealed tank confirms that the unit is functioning well.

He pops the lid of the compartment, revealing stirring water and the shapes of the dark clams. They are bunched up; he knows he must get them out and into the sun as soon as he can to allow them to feed. He knows that

he must construct them a new home by morning. To deprive
and light for any longer will mean the end.

He looks up to the sun now hovering above the cliff on t
the lake. In thirty minutes this little bowl will be in shadow, and
after that it will be too dark to see. Even though he has only slept in snatches the last three nights, now is not the time for rest. He drags the cart out of the shadow of the cliff. At least the clams in the top layer will eat the day's last light.

He turns to the load still trussed in the tarpaulin. Inside he has the recirculation system for one of Mocke's abalone pits which he will modify to his purposes, and he has twenty kilograms of Fritz Reef Mix to salt the water in which he will grow his creatures.

He cannot waste time. He must construct the tank in which the clams will lie separate from the lake, and the recirculation chamber, and then he must fill the tank and sand it and salt it, and then he must place his clams in their new home so that they can begin to feed on the rising sun – all of this by morning. When that is done, he must build the second tank, for the Baai will not be saved unless they can breed.

On impulse he turns to the silent water behind him, looking for the creature. But the lake is empty and the cliff stares back. He looks to the tangle of trees on the western shore. Nothing.

She will come to him; there is nowhere else for her to go. First, he must complete his task.

He turns to the load and begins.

That night the clatter of Uncle Mike's generator echoes across the pool, bouncing from the sheer cliffs and sailing up into the night. Two of his work lights are strung up from the cart. They cast a pool of white light in which he toils. Unused to the noise, the creatures of the pool look on – the rock rabbits peer from their ledges and the frogs watch from the shallows, while from beneath the waterfall she is watching him also, and drinking his thoughts.

She cannot look away. He stalks through the jumble of his building site.

ets of wood lie scattered as he cuts them to shape with a giant blade, and s time flows through the night he assembles what seems to be some kind of box, growing on the rocky shore. He saws and hammers and paints, and at times sits staring at the stars, and then begins again. All through the night she watches him work, seeing him grow gaunt. It is near to morning when suddenly the clatter of the little generator disappears. The silence is shocking. She sees his head jerk up at the sudden calm, and then turn to the east where faintly the outline of the mountain can be seen. He shakes his great head and strides to the scattered pile of his belongings. He bends and then a beam of light comes arcing from his hand.

With the torch he returns to his work, spreading paint over the box he has built, over and over. She shifts in the water, drawing on the peace of the liquid, and the mayhem of the life of the riverbank. Here are roots twisting through soil and branches twisting through air, and the breathing of the weavers and the doves, and frogs and snakes and fish. She is aware of them all. Their dreaming settles on her shoulders, her fingers curl among the roots.

Morning has risen by the time his tank is complete. He cannot comprehend the night's labour. From the moment he made the decision to leave the Baai he had known how crucial this night would be. He had set himself the target of placing the clams by morning, this being the fourth day of them having had no sun from which to feed, but he had also known that his goal was unlikely, perhaps impossible. Just as pulling the cart over the mountain was impossible. And now he sits beside a tank that is not yet ready. He has coated the whole structure with sealant. It is quick-drying, but he knows it will still be hours before he can home the clams. He shakes his tired head. What he needs is space, for his clams to breathe, and space for them to feel the sun and eat it. And he needs salt water. He shakes his tired brain. Something is pulling at him, some idea.

Suddenly, he jerks upright. *The tarp!*

Again he shakes his head, washing the fog away. He had earmarked the tarp for use later as a seedbed, and initially as a rain cover, but he could just as easily use it now. 'Stupid,' he mutters, smacking his ear and rising.

He lumbers to his materials, seeing clearly a vision of what he must do: the big blue tarp spread inside the still drying tank, forming a tank within a tank, so that the still wet epoxy can dry beneath. As he stumbles to the tank with the tarp trailing behind him, the sun crests the cliff above. He shivers. Yes. This is what they all need. Sun.

'It will be a miracle if they survive,' he mutters as he begins spreading the tarp inside the tank. He is aware of every potential pitfall, from infection to leakage to recirculation to incorrect salination, and yet he continues. 'They will survive,' he tells himself as he spreads the heavy tarp. 'They must.'

Night. She is within the lake, her back to the cliff directly across from his campsite. Only her head is above the water that has become her home. She has eaten the fish of the lake; she has rested in its womb and she is refreshed. And she watches. The box the man has built is barely visible in the night, as is his body that lies seemingly dead half in and half out of the water, his face to the rock. His snores rumble in the water.

Moonrise.

She looks to the orb rising above the cliff. Tonight it will be full, and there will be shadows.

'*Eat*,' she sounds, as she pushes off into the lake. The deep water is glorious, as are the creatures turning within. Her goal is the box lying stark and square on the rock.

She glides through the dark water, approaching it and the sleeping man. She can see now that he lies on his cheek with his face towards her. His eyes are folded away beneath the deep wrinkles of his eyelids and the labour of the last few days. His face is swollen, his cheeks rashed with new beard, his mouth like a fruit, crumpled and parted. His chin is caught between the bone of his skull, the mountain beneath it and the pad of his shoulder.

Her fingers touch the bottom of the lake. She slides toward him in the water. There is much she wants to see.

She crawls dripping from the lake, keeping the box between her and him. She looks inside it. The tarpaulin tumbles around its lip. Carefully she walks beside it, using her hands on it to take the weight off of her shattered legs.

She had watched him toil all afternoon, lifting buckets from the lake and splashing them into his bed of tarp while his machine assisted, splurging the water from the lake into the deepening aquarium. She watched him spooning powder into the box and saw him taking measurements with a metal object as he rode his weariness. She saw him scowl and calculate and hesitate at the amount of powder he added, and finally he had sat and sunk his head between his knees, and then with weariness stood and began removing the clams from the cart and placing them into the new water.

And now she looks into that water as the moon rises, and within it she sees twelve of them at rest. Her clams. As the moonlight enters the water, two open their shells, tasting this memory of the sun.

She is near the far end of the box where a noisy machine whirs. Two dark snakes extend from it into the water and from them a current circulates throughout the tank. She understands. The clams need movement, water must pass through their gills.

She puts her finger into the water, and then her hand. She reaches down to place her palm on the shell of the clam below her.

The animal is dying, its thoughts are faint and growing fainter. All are dying. She leans forward, letting her arm and then her torso and then her whole body slide into the water. The salt of it is soothing. She takes a breath and sinks beneath. Immediately the sound of the pump is altered, echoing within her head, thumping, booming, and the thoughts of her clams come to her more strongly. She lays her body on top of them, touching all with her bare flesh. She trails her fingers across them, caressing their open mouths and exposed mantles, stirring them back to life. The feet of the clams emerge, tasting their mother. She sings to them and in her ears, slowly, they begin to sing in return.

'*My children are hungry*.'

And she feeds them.

A wave rises from her womb and surges through her. It washes against her throat and sucks with the tide back to her centre, where it circulates.

She parts her legs and a milky cloud trails from her into the water, bathing the lips of each exposed clam.

She croons, singing to the plankton as they settle and fill her children with the nutrients they need.

Lovingly she arranges them, turning their mouths to the coming sun, orientating them to the current as is their preference, and soothing them with her care. Their feet dance in the moonlight.

As the clams are enriched by their mother, so she is enriched by them. She opens her eyes beneath the water and allows tears to flow, sending waves of song to take the tears and wipe them across every smiling mantle and every dancing foot. She croons at the pleasure of home.

She stays this way for hours, singing with her children, breathing nothing but them.

As dawn nears, it is time to leave. She sighs and gathers herself, readying herself for the weight of the world out there. She lowers her feet to the bottom of the tank and stands, rising into the frigid night air.

She had almost forgotten it, this new world. She stands dripping beneath the moon, and she is grateful. She looks up to the heavens and despite the glow of the moon up there some of the stars still shine. Near the horizon is the belt of the hunter. She looks for the scorpion, craning her to neck to find its sting, but it is not yet raised in the still summer skies. She drinks the stars, and is glad they did not take her that night on the mountain. They are her friends; they are the memory of her love.

She sighs. How will she find him in this endless and uncertain place? She cannot hear him, she cannot feel him, the abyss between them is great. She wonders if he is gone from her. Will she ever see him again? She sends her question to the stars and they answer: 'Yes.'

She nods at the truth of it, at the truth of the solidity of her own body and her own breath plunging through her.

She looks to her left where the man lies on the ground, taking the opportunity to study him up close without his knowing. His head is turned away from her. She studies the line of cropped hair against his neck, the intimacy of his ear turned to the moon, the skin behind it. She listens to his laboured breathing, the snore sawing from his obstructed throat.

There are scars on his back. Their pucker shines wet beneath the moon. They twist across him, innumerable cuts and ridges collected over the years. His right arm is thrust toward her, laid dead across the rock of the mountain, the palm upward and the fingers splayed open. His hands are giant, his wrist as thick as a stalk of fleshy kelp. Blood is streaked on his forearm. Lines painted black lead to the cut she observed that night. It lies like a swollen fruit. The lips of the wound have not sealed and the flesh has risen up, swallowing the stitches so that they are now cutting into the skin.

Intrigued, she steps out of the tank he has built, placing her new foot on the mountain. Quietly she steps toward him, watching for his waking, but he is dead to the world. She crouches next to him and brings her face close to the wound. Infection. She can smell it. The flesh is red and purple. She closes her eyes and feels the pulse of heat spreading from it, to the beat of his heart. She places her hand over it. He moans. She tastes the sound of that moan, letting it circulate inside her. She opens her eyes and again studies the cut. She touches the lips of it with her fingers, taking in the spikes of gut caught in the swollen flesh, pricking her skin. And then she trails her fingers down the flesh of his forearm, to the branch of his wrist, to the yam of his swollen hand. She puts her face to his fingers, studying them. They too are swollen. From work, the infection and dehydration. The nail of his thumb has been ripped in two by his hammer, the pads of his fingers and palm are alternately shredded or worked to leather. She sees these swollen fingers and imagines this beast trying to sew his arm together.

She giggles to herself.

She goes to explore his camping place. Her eyes feast on everything he has brought. Every tool, every twist of wire, every clamp and every shred of cloth dragged across a mountain. What a strange creature, she thinks, turning to look at him. He is nothing like her love.

Jono is gentle, even his hunting is done with grace, and his heart is one of peace. This man. She looks at his scars, and she hears his moaning. He is driven by a storm, while Jono is driven by a breeze.

Even from here she can feel the heat of the wound. She turns to his equipment and searches through it. She remembers many of these items from her day in the boy's hut, and she remembers how he had repaired his stitches after she had ripped them open. She searches through the piles of all he has brought, the boxes and tools and rope and tarp and wood, hammer and saw and brush and bucket, until finally she sees what she is looking for, lying on top of a red tin box, the one that stood outside her love's door. A silver blade with a blue handle. She picks it up and returns to the sleeping man. She eyes the smooth of his neck beneath his ear, where an artery pulses. How easy it would be to cut his throat. She places the blade there, watching the soft throbbing beneath the steel, and she remembers. *Let him suffer.* She crouches again to his wound. She extends the blade under the moon, and sinks it into the swollen lips, pressing against the steel of the strands of gut, and feeling the release as one after another parts under the knife. The man groans as the wound pops open. She knows he will not wake, even though his groans deepen and his body twitches.

She watches the wound empty itself, and listens as the breathing of the man evens. '*What a strange creature*,' she thinks, looking on this being so alone in the mountains.

CHAPTER TWELVE

The man does not wake for two days. For two days she prowls her valley, and her lake, and his equipment, and makes all of it hers. On her creaking legs she moves through his place. The piles and drifts of it shift to orderly lines and every item is blessed with her gaze. Soon she knows every piece that is here, and every creature that inhabits the lake, and every rabbit that scampers now unafraid before her. As she explores this rocky bowl held high in the mountains, she is drawn again and again to the mountain of him lying at the edge of the water, his feet sodden. She watches the wound as first it dries in the noon sun and then scabs over. But still, she knows it is not healed. There are times when she places her nose near to it and inhales, and the scent of infection is there. At night she returns to her clams, slumbering with them beneath the waning moon.

When he finally wakes he stumbles to the tank, thinking only '*Do they live?*' The pump is intact and whirring, the solar panels are still powering it night and day. He reaches the lip of his box and peers over the edge. The water is circulating, pristine, and the clams crouch in ordered rows. He stares. He did not lay them like this. Each of their lips are parted and their mantles flash blue and orange fluorescence. Each of them is thriving, beaming and open to the sun.

He turns to look over his shoulder to the burning sphere above.

'Too much,' he mutters as he lurches to his equipment, hobbling against the life flowing back into his waterlogged feet. 'Need shade.'

Nothing is as he remembered it. Quickly he sifts through the piles of his equipment, finding his big fold of green netting. He throws it out, grunting at the pain in his back and legs, the old weather-stiffened net raining muck. He drags it across rock and sand and heaves it over the lip, sand falling into the clear water as the burn of the high sun recedes. Again he looks over his shoulder to the fiery orb, lips parched.

He scowls.

He tramps to the edge of the trees where he finds four stout branches. He hacks them from the undergrowth and drags them back to his prize. With long spikes he hammers them into the edge of the tank and then one by one, he raises the net to make an awning. Finally, it is done.

His thirst awakens. Without a thought he stumbles forward into the water, and as he takes off from the shelf and falls in a churn of bubbles, he opens his mouth and drinks. He opens his eyes and washes them, and he opens his arms and lets the water soothe his burning back. Minutes later he returns to the shelf, blowing, and heaves himself onto it.

He thinks of hunger and feels it. Such appetite! He notes the rifle and bullets in his pack and imagines a rabbit turning over a fire. Juice floods his mouth. He grins through the water beaded in his beard. It is good to be hungry, good to have appetite. Absently the fingers of his right hand wander to the crook of his left, looking for the slice and the steel spikes of gut that he has come to know. But the gut is gone.

He prods it carefully. It has split open and has scabbed over but for a hole at the centre. It is cool to the touch.

He smiles. The gut must have split and he has been given this gift. He clamps the nails of his forefinger and thumb onto the knot of the gut still spiking out of his flesh. He pulls and the black thread slides out easy and clean. He takes the gut at the other end of the wound where it is still caught. That too slides out easy and clean.

He sniffs the gut. He scowls. No, not clean. Something lingers.

He peers at the wound. He wipes it open, splitting part of the scab. The flesh within is pink but tender. And right in the centre is a dark spot. He sniffs at it. There is something in there.

He turns to his campsite.

The boy's knife, where is it?

A pail of water bubbles over his fire with his hunting blade within it. He sits easy. He knows what he must do.

'I should have antibiotics,' he mutters as he removes the steaming blade, his calloused fingers only dimly feeling the heat. He does however have ethanol, and the wound shines with the liquid's sting. He angles his arm to the sun, maximising the light, and peers again at the dark spot in there, just beneath the flesh. He brings his blade nearer and carefully lets the bright edge pierce the surface. He pushes it in, his scowl the only sign of discomfort, looking for the hard edge of the black. But the blade does not find it. He grunts. He pushes the blade deeper, slicing left and right and angling down, sure that the object must be just there, and at any moment his blade will hook its edge. Blood starts to well from the open cut. Already he has sunk his blade two centimetres into his arm. He shakes his head and pulls the blade out.

He reaches for his bottle of ethanol and allows some of it to fall into the wound. The sting sets his scowl. Whatever is within will not come out.

'So be it,' he murmurs, and sits back from the fire.

He looks around, to his lake, and the cliff, and finally to the trees. This bowl of water high in the mountain regards him in return, impassive. He rises, a gesture of defiance against even these cliffs that he would call home. He knows that there is no sympathy here, that man and beast receive only what they are allocated, and when their account is due there is no reprieve. He stalks down to his equipment and tools, ready to continue his work.

That night a fire crackles on the edge of the lake. He sits beside it, two rock rabbits blackening on sticks above. The birds of the trees are silent; only the waterfall speaks. He looks out over the dark water.

Where is she?

He searches the shallows, carefully drawing his eyes around all of the edge. There are innumerable crevices for her to hide in, innumerable shadows in which to crouch.

By now he has examined the clams. They are in better health than he could have hoped for. With his hydrometer he has tested the salinity of the water and found it at a level of perfection that he could not have achieved. He has returned the tarp, placing the clams in their new tank that is now sealed with epoxy. He has begun to lay out the foundation of his new seedbed in the shallows. It is risky, but he will have to use this second tank to drain the water into, so that he might move his main tank down to the shallows.

He rests in the knowledge of his work completed, and in the knowledge of her. He knows that she has saved them, and that she ministered to his wound. And he knows this place is different. In the time that he slept something has changed. The song of the birds is different, the lapping of the water is different. The roar of the waterfall, a sound he has known for many days and nights, has changed.

He shifts his eyes to the dark smear of the trees, and he knows.

She is the difference. This valley has taken on new life.

It is the same as hunting sailfish and feeling that snap on the line. Where before there was open and empty ocean now there is certainty, a relationship, for the creature is here.

Soon his rabbits are cooked and he eats them, the first food for many days, and soon his fire has burned low and still he sits watching the dark water. He knows she has saved them. He knows she is out there.

And so he waits.

And finally, she comes.

A shiver heralds her arrival, the softest breeze upon his cheek. In the dark water he sees a white smudge blooming. Ripples extend from it, circling outward, the centre travelling towards him until she rises. He watches her eyes appear, fixed on him.

Carefully, she stands. Her form assaults him. She has grown. In the half-light he cannot be certain, but it seems that she is a foot taller, and her legs are finely muscled. He remembers the feel of her shins beneath his fingers, the fine fractures running through the bone.

She pauses at the edge of the water.

Why is she waiting? Is she looking at him? He cannot see the direction of her gaze or the blaze of her eyes. But the embers of the fire are bright, his position clear.

She pauses a moment more at the edge, steadying herself it seems, and then she glides over the rocky ground to the tank. Her long silhouette flickers in the gloom. A moment more he watches her, a regal shadow within shadow, and then she slips into the tank.

He stares at the box in the moonlight, imagining the creature within.

'*What are you doing with my clams?*'

The words are shocking. He has heard them as he hears his own mind – it is the sound of his own voice, but its origin is not the same. The words come from outside him, he is certain. They come from her.

His throat is dry. He swallows, and then he speaks to the dark.

'I am growing pearls with them. I will use them to save the Baai.'

The silence echoes back at him. The waterfall clatters to the lake, the moon beams, and the warm night is a whisper.

He doubts himself. He prepares to put this voice he has heard aside, and then it speaks again with a clarity that burns.

'*You may.*'

The words are as clear as is if she were sitting beside him.

He does not reply. Instead, he sits beside his faintly glowing coals, drinking the night.

In the morning he takes time to ensure that she is not there. He is noisy at making his fire and brewing his coffee, he is loud at going a little way into the trees to relieve himself. He is sure she has gone when he finally approaches the tank. But still he approaches cautiously, his heart hammering as he peers in under the awning and sees that she is not there.

The clams are there. Two perfect rows of them, with shells open and mantles greedily awaiting the sun. He passes his hand across the top of them and they close one by one at his shadow. He dips a cleaned paint tin into the tank and raises it up. Softly he places his spectacles on his nose and carefully inserts his thermometer into the sample, taking a reading, and then he places his hydrometer inside. He waits as the gauge rises. Soon he has a number. He checks it against his plastic-wrapped table, and scratches at his temple as he calculates. 1.022. Once again, perfect.

He is about to leave the tank, his day's work beckoning, when something catches his eye. The shell of the clam just beneath him. Clustered along the sweep of it is a rash so fine he almost missed it, a moss mottled to the same black as the shell. Alarmed, Uncle Mike thrusts his nose closer. An infection is the last thing he needs. And then his breathing pauses in his throat. The mottled growth is not some alien, they are in fact tiny clams, little veliger, each with its own gossamer shell and the beginnings of a foot.

They have bred.

He turns his eyes to the others and carefully examines their shells. Everywhere, on every sweep of every surface is the same dark rash. On every shell are clusters of veliger, hundreds of baby clams.

He rears up, searching the lake, the riven cliffs and the jumbled treeline.

She is nowhere.

Hope rises in him; certainty steals into his heart. Although impossible, he feels his enterprise will succeed. And why not? Why would this blessed bowl high in the mountain not once again provide a miracle? He purses his lips and begins to whistle while he sets to work making the second of his tanks.

'Every man gets his chance,' he mutters. 'Yes. Every man.'

But his optimism is tempered by the throbbing of his arm. The black seed pulses within.

He works feverishly. Having already completed one tank he begins to cut from memory, trusting instinct to mark and saw so that he may keep his momentum. He ploughs through the remaining wood, calculating what is left of the materials he has. He wants a bigger tank than the first. He believes he has the sealant, piping, awning and tubing necessary.

While he works he allows thoughts of returning to the Baai for resupply to rise in his mind, as well as the option of taking the trail further east and journeying to a neighbouring settlement to find his wares. But his labours are procrastinations, his circling dreams attempts at keeping reality at bay. What was at first a sense has become sensation. Fever is rising in his cells. His movements are becoming heavier; he is beginning to swim through mud. The dark seed in his wound is now also in his brain. It grows there; it is doubt.

He soldiers on until it is time to assemble his first two panels into base and wall. Immediately he sees that his workmanship is incorrect. He has not cut cleanly; his first edge is not flush. 'I'll file it down,' he tuts and mutters, and then chuckles at that idea. His tank requires precision. He does not have silicone to hide imperfections.

'I'll use the tarp,' he murmurs, putting his hand out to wood to steady himself, and again laughter is his answer. He knows this is not a good path. To rely on the tarp as a tank in case he makes a mistake is to accept imperfections. He cannot waste anything out here; he can't afford mistakes. A sudden spike of fever runs through him, and he knows he must quit.

'We have twelve,' he mutters as he seats himself on the rock. 'She will care for them.'

He looks at his arm. The cut is inflamed, swollen against his skin. He shakes his head; he knows he cannot dig there again. It is the digging that has aggravated the wound.

Heat rises.

He looks to the lake and the cool water. He is afraid to go in there. He might lose consciousness and drown. He sits a moment, feeling the pull of the forest to his right but not wanting to look. But he must. He knows he has to take shelter inside. This is not what he had wanted; he meant to have finished his work before entering that place, but fate has played his hand.

'Perhaps it is time,' he muses as he groans to his feet.

Fever is bending time; every movement is an effort. He begins to shuffle. He goes with his hands held out to preserve his balance, inching his way forward while the infection rises.

It is cool in the forest. Against his building fever the dappled shade brings relief. Sound is muted here. He stands for a moment, listening, looking. The fever is giving him a heightened clarity. He sees the trees in hyper detail. 'They are the same,' he mutters, reaching out to place his hand against the long neck of one. They twist ahead to form a path, the same path he has known before.

He shuffles forward, pulling himself with sloth-like hands from bough to bough, his bare feet sinking amongst soft leaves. The world is green and sinuous brown; the low forest holds him in its heart.

'*She brought me here, it was not me*,' he mutters. '*I did as you asked me. I did everything you asked me.*'

His arm throbs. It has been twenty long years since last he trod this way. Twenty years of waiting to return.

He concentrates on his hands, one in front of the other, one to grasp before releasing the one behind, pulling himself deeper into the trees, deeper into fever. He slides through them like a great chameleon.

'*This could be it*,' he mutters, steeling himself to face his ever companion. He hears singing. The voice is dancing among the leaves. He can see the place through the trees now. There is the meadow. The singing is warbling from there.

He moves through like a bear, a great ghost without sound. And now he sees the source of the song. The creature is there, the girl. 'Like a bee to honey,' he mutters, sure that he is the bee.

The creature is in the clearing, held by the soft grass of the meadow. There is a stone planted in the earth at her head. She is on her knees, a stick clutched in both hands, and she is digging.

He stops to look at her. Her voice fills the air and at the same time turns in his chest. It burns. He does not want to break her peace, but of course he must: this is his trajectory.

'What are you digging for?'

She does not turn to look at him, instead she continues.

'*I don't know. There is something buried here.*'

'*I don't want you to dig in there. This place is precious to me.*'

'This is not your place, it is mine.'

He comes to stand beside her.

'Will you help me?'

She turns to him and he is struck by her eyes. It occurs to him that if he were to depart now, he would be happy. He holds his arm out to her. It is a tuber swelling from his elbow, fat and purple.

She turns her eyes to the cut. The lips of it are black. She touches it with her fingertips. His body shivers.

'What is buried here?'

'My wife is buried in this ground.'

She places her thumbs on either side of the wound, and still she looks into his eyes.

'She has been long dead.'

'Yes.'

'But she did not die here.'

'No.'

'She died in the Baai, away from here. And you brought her back. You dragged her over the mountain.'

'Yes, I brought her home.'

She continues to look into him, deeper. He can feel her moving inside him. He begins to shiver.

'But she is not the only one buried here.'

'No.'

'There is a tiny box. Who does it belong to?'

'It was our daughter's.'

'That is the one I want. She is the secret you are hiding from me.'

She presses the flesh and the wound distends. He writhes against her fingers, but he does not move away. In his gasping she sees a dark-haired little girl. His whole heart, walking in the world.

'I will tell you all of it.'

She shifts her thumbs down to catch the underside of the bulb, the wound's black lips swelling up and parting as she presses.

He looks into her green eyes, the fever causing them to blaze.

She bears down on the wound, taking delight in digging her fingers beneath the awful fruit until finally its black throat appears, a tiny yellow dot distending at its mouth.

Sweat is pouring from him.

'*You are hiding something, but I will discover the truth. I will pull it out of you.*'

She pushes, and then it tears and pus gluts from the opening.

The man gasps and faints.

She looks on him for a moment, this fallen bear in the woods, then she inspects the wound, palpating it with her fingers, releasing milky blood. There is an open chamber beneath the fluid. She inserts her finger into it, probing as the big man twitches beneath her. She spits into the wound, cleaning it, and spreads the lips of it apart. She blows gently on the flesh, soothing it, probing it, and then she spies its secret. A grain of black. Gently she coaxes, stroking at the seed with her fingertip until finally it emerges at the lip. A piece of flesh. She raises it to her eye. It is from the cephalopod.

'*Great mother*,' she sounds to the shred of meat.

She places it in her wet mouth and swallows.

She sits for a time, cross-legged beside the giant body, looking out on this clearing in the wood.

CHAPTER THIRTEEN

He wakes in the night, stirring to the sounds of trees. He is light; the fever has gone. He raises his arm. There is pain but the swelling is gone also. He eyes the wound, a scabbing mouth in the dark. He turns onto his side and finds not a mound but an open hole beside him, the gravestone cast aside. He exclaims, and then exhaustion claims him.

He wakes again with pain in his cheek, his face pressed to the stone. There is a rustling breeze in the trees, and before him dank and turned earth.

He can smell it.

He struggles to his knees.

The waning moon shines through the canopy, revealing an excavation. He leans forward to put his hand into the cold of the hole. His fingers explore that dark, feeling nothing but collapsed earth. The little box is gone.

He places his flat palm on the earth at the bottom for a time, breathing. And then he begins to dig. It does not take him long. Soon his fingers are touching wood. He cannot help himself. He widens the hole, scooping the earth aside with his giant hands, making it large enough for his head and torso. He crawls down into the soil and places his cheek against the wood.

'*My love,*' he whispers. But the wood does not speak, and the bones within are silent.

He does not mind, he has long since made peace with the silence. He enlarges the hole, scraping the dirt away, finding the extent of the coffin within the ground. He glories in it, the soil upon his skin, the worms and the insects beneath the waning moon, and her in her box with him. Within the ground is seepage from the lake. The moisture coats him as he lies with his love in the earth.

And then a voice croaks. The moisture moves about him, and suddenly he does not know if he lies upon the coffin among the worms and the beetles, or if he has been spirited to another place. For it is black about him, covering him; water or soil, it makes no difference. He has been taken from the world. It is her, he knows it. She has taken him. This soil is her soil, the water is her water. It is from here that the creatures of this valley know her, that she speaks with them. But the grave is not hers, he knows that also, the bones are not hers, and he holds onto that knowledge with all his might.

Something passes his legs. She is inside him. He closes his eyes and sees with her sight. In her arms she clutches the box. She opens it. Inside there are the items of a young girl. A red comb made from horsehair and wood, the paint faded. A blanket tucked in, frayed by the years, and the carved figure of a fish.

'*Where is she? There is no body in here.*'

'Her body was lost. These were her treasured things.'

Her fingers enter the box and whisper through the folds of the blanket. They take up the carved fish. She fixes him with her green eyes.

'*Where was her body lost?*'

Her face is impassive, her mouth unmoving, but her voice sounds in his mind.

'She was drowned at sea. I searched for her for many days.'

He does not look away from her furious eyes, even though they cripple him. Her fingers stroke the scales of the carved fish.

'*She is the source of your guilt.*'

'Yes.'

'*You killed her.*'

'No.'

'But it was by your fault that she died.'

'Yes.'

'Why?'

He feels her moving inside him, searching for his secrets, turning his heart upside down. He clings to the coffin, knowing that in this kingdom of soil and water all is hers, but for this wood, these bones, this love. If he can hold it in his mind, remember it, he will not be obliterated.

But she is relentless. She is peeling him apart. Her face begins to change, becoming a mask of hatred. Shivers cascade up his spine. For her face is an image from his own past.

'She looked at you like this,' whispers the creature, a sound so slight it is all he can hear. *'She hated you. Why?'*

Uncle Mike can hardly draw breath, so awesome is her fury leering down at him.

'She loved a man who I would not allow.'

'Why?'

'I did not think him worthy.'

She covers the sky above him, her eight limbs at work throughout his flesh, testing the truth of his words.

'There was an accident on the sea. Her husband fell from their boat. He was snared in his own lines. He sank, and she dived to follow him.'

'She dived to escape you.'

The words of the creature echo with eternity. He cannot deny them.

'Yes.'

'Did your wife have hatred for you?'

'No. There was nothing between us but love.'

'But your daughter had hatred for you. Why?'

He does not speak.

'Say it. Tell me why.'

'Because I would not set her free.'

There is silence, as the endless worlds hear his admission.

'Yes, that is why.'

The creature relents, the pressure about him subsides, and his fingers cease their clawing on the wood. The stars return to the heavens, and he finds himself returned to the earth.

'You would not set her free, and now she is gone from you forever.'

The bear nods and then he turns his face to the crook of his arm and weeps, shielding his tears from the world.

The sun is rising when he comes from the forest. The campsite seems empty, but soon he spies a foot emerging from the lip of the first tank. She is inside.

He goes to collect his rifle and quickly shoots a rabbit on the cliff above. He returns to his camping place where he begins to light a fire.

'What was she like?'

He pauses at the feeling of her words. It is marvellous to him. Like a memory they fade when he attempts to pinpoint them, but they are clear now.

He sets about skinning the rabbit.

'She was like her mother. Proud and strong. And like her father. Defiant.'

'Am I like her?'

He skewers the animal and places it above the flames.

'Yes, you are like her. You are beautiful and alone, like her.'

'Am I her?'

'No.'

'When you first saw me, you thought I was her.'

'You came from the sea. I wished God had brought her back to me. But you are not her.'

'Who am I?'

'I do not know. Only God knows.'

He hears a stirring in the tank and turns as she emerges. She has grown taller; she is now as tall as he.

'She liked to sit on my shoulders. I would walk in the surf with her, on the beach, with the spray splashing us both. She loved the sea, like her mother.'

She is picking her way across the rock towards him. Her steps are surer now, her legs strong.

'You do not love the sea?'

'No. I was born in these mountains, but far from here. I loved them, and they the sea. Now the sea is my reminder of them.'

'*They were from the Baai?*'

He shakes his head.

'All of us were outsiders to the Baai. I come from these mountains, and my wife from another place beside the sea, far to the north. There was a war when we were young. We both were thrown from our homes. We found each other in these mountains.'

She drops her head, listening to the histories in his words.

'My wife and I spent many months at this lake when we were young, hiding from the war. This is where we found our life together. Where our daughter was conceived.'

'Your wife loved to be beneath the trees.'

'Yes. And she loved this lake. She was like you; she swam like a fish.' He stares into the flames. 'That is why I brought my daughter here, to be with her mother. So that she may finally rest in the peace of the trees.'

'*She did not have peace?*'

'No. She was violent. Only her mother brought her peace. But her mother died when she was very young.'

'*If the trees and the lake were her place, what is yours?*'

He gestures up the cliff and beyond it, to the slopes of the mountain rising above them.

'I like the open spaces, and the cool wind. I like to see far.'

He reaches forward to slice some of the meat off of the rabbit.

'Will you eat?' he asks her.

She shakes her head, but watches as he does. There is something in him that reminds her of Jonothan. While this man is bullish, both are careful. He slices the meat carefully, not wanting to waste it, and he chews it thoughtfully.

'*Why do you hate Jonothan?*'

'I don't hate him. I just wish...' He shakes his head. 'He is asleep, a dreamer. This world does not have sympathy for dreamers. I want him to wake up.'

'Why did he wound you?'

He looks up and sees the pain in her eyes.

'I saved him from drowning. He cut me and ran. I am not surprised. That is what I expect of him.'

The fire crackles as the flames eat the remaining wood. He feeds them another twisting branch.

'Is he alive?'

'He knows how to live off the sea. I am sure he is alive.'

'You did not hurt him?'

He spreads his arms to her, showing his open hands and the open cut on his arm.

'I did not hurt him.'

He drops his hands and looks to the rock beneath his feet. He shakes his head. 'Come,' he says suddenly, 'I have something that you will like. Let us have peace.'

He turns the rabbit carcass away from the fire.

'Come.' He raises his eyes to her. 'Let me show you.'

He holds out his hand.

'Please.'

His eyes are full of these mountains.

'Come.'

She does not take his hand but she does follow him as he walks back up the track and then turns to the cliff, climbing up and over onto the slope of the mountain beyond. He turns once up there, dropping his hand down for her to take.

'Let me show you.'

She puts her palm in his and he raises her up to the slope.

She follows him as he strides ahead among the low bush of the mountain-side. Up here the world is a tumult of distance. At every angle is vista upon vista, distant peaks in blue and lighter blue and grey, fading to a horizon curving across the world. She feels exposed; there is nothing between here and the kingdom of the sun. A fresh wind is blowing. It ripples the tops of the low bushes and the dark hair of the man climbing the slope before her.

She can see that this is his home. He lopes upwards, as if there is no gradient and no force of gravity to unstick them from this place beneath the sky.

'Come,' he gestures, smiling.

He kneels down, placing his hands among the bushes. 'Come,' he says again.

She sinks down next to him, grateful to be nearer the rock.

'Here I am alone,' he tells her, his face split by a smile as fresh as the wind that plays about them. 'Here, I am free.'

He gestures around him to the peaks and the wide sky sinking to the blaze of sunset. He closes his eyes to them and the wind. 'It is only us.'

He strokes a cluster of lightly pink and purple flowers that dance on their stalks. He allows them to brush his fingers and then he invites her hand to touch them also. '*Konkelboom*,' he tells her.

She immerses her fingers in them, allowing them to dance against her skin, and then down past the soft of their blossoms to the woody stalks beneath.

'As children we would eat these.'

Gently he digs at their base, taking hold of their stalks and pulling while he massages the soil away with the tips of his fingers and knuckles.

'Look. Dig gently around their stalks, you will see, the fruit is hidden.'

Softly, the plant begins to crumble up and out of the soil, revealing a tuberous root system. Uncle Mike follows the revealed tuber with his fingers, working it carefully from the soil. Soon he has unearthed a string of tubers each the size of the pad of his little finger.

'Gently,' he tells her, 'there is more here than you could ever eat.'

He continues to dig and worry at the soil while he breathes the wind and looks out to the blazing sky. He plucks one of the little fruits from the roots he holds, and with his knife pares a strip of skin away. White flesh is revealed beneath, tinged with pink. He carves a slice of it and holds it out to her.

'Taste.'

She does, accepting the sliver of clean fruit and placing it on her tongue. It is lightly bitter. As bitter as the bite of the fresh wind and the sharpness of this elevated air. As bitter as a height attained that extends no further, and as sweet. The flavour washes her mouth.

'*I like it.*'

He nods, and grins, looking out onto the faraway world.

'There,' he says, pointing to the hazy west, 'there is the Baai. Can you see it?'

She looks out and finds the river of the trail that they followed as it twists through the long mountain, but she cannot see the little town.

'*It is too far away.*'

'But it is there.'

He carves a sliver of the fruit for himself; a drop only on his large finger, but the pleasure of that childhood taste is full.

He raises his hand, pointing out to the north. 'The last I saw the boy, he went there.'

She turns to the distant coast, nothing but a haze on the edge of the world.

'He knows the land out there. He has fished there many times. I would not worry. This world is large, but the heart does not forget its way home.'

She turns her eye to him as he looks out. He has taken on the character of the mountain. This endless vista and these infinite gradations of colour are washed across his face. He is a part of this peak, as surely as the rocks themselves or the little bushes around them.

It is dark when they make their way down the mountainside. About each of them is peace. He can hear nothing but the sound of her footfalls, and she, she sees nothing but his great silhouette against the rising stars.

'Let us do it now,' he says when they have returned to their camp. He looks among his tools and takes up a tiny white-painted box. 'Will you help me?'

'*What will you do?*'

'Impregnate our clams, so that they are with pearl.'

He clicks his torch, the light spraying across the camp, revealing the rabbit still hung near the fire, his rolled sleeping mat, his jumbled tools in their piles. He strides toward the tank, and she follows.

'I have not done this myself before, but I have studied it. I believe I can do it.'

He spreads a section of tarp onto the bare rock and places his little toolbox on top of it.

His torchlight pierces the clear water of the main tank, revealing the twelve clams in their rows. He plays his torch over them. With the sun gone their shells are closed and the torchlight is a rude intrusion. Uncle Mike reaches his hand into the water, his arm bending by refraction as his fingers grasp the first clam. He lifts the animal from its place in the sand, streaming water.

'We must implant one of my beads.'

He shows her with his meaty finger, stroking at the lip of the animal's shell. 'I will use an implement to place it inside here. The clam will then cover the bead with its excretion, making our pearl.'

He kneels to place the clam on the tarp, and beside it he opens his tool box.

She looks down on his collection of tweezers and wedges.

'We will place one bead in each clam, and slowly, with each pearl, we will buy the Baai its freedom.'

She kneels and places her hand on the shell of the animal, a clear sign for him to pause.

She lifts the animal and turns to the tank. One foot after the other she climbs into it, lowering herself until she is sitting on the sand and her body is covered by the water. He follows her movements with his torch, emboldened when she does not disagree. He lights the clam in her hands, watching as she places it in her lap. She leans forward, allowing her head to sink below the water, and one by one she gathers the clams laid out ahead of her, and places them all in a pile before her. He marvels as their shells begin to open and their feet emerge, tasting the water around her.

Her head breaks the surface and she looks up to him.

'*Come*' is her unmistakable message. He must obey.

He steps into the tank, his bulk taking up all available space, and as he lowers himself the water rises over the lip and washes over the side.

He is uncertain.

She places her feet on his, her creatures clustered between his feet too. She leans her head back against the lip of the tank, the first clam still held in her lap, and closes her eyes. She begins to hum while she caresses the creature. He watches her in the last gloom of day, and then closes his eyes also.

Now his mind is free to roam. He listens to her humming. Her feet begin to warm, imperceptibly but steadily. Her humming circles around him gently, like the tide rising and falling through the caves of the seaside. He feels the song is washing him, inside and out.

His mind begins to wander. Moments arise out of the black, precise points in his own history. A boy and he at play in the mountains. Suddenly the boy is on the ground with blood on his lip and eyes full of pain. He regards this lost boy, and somehow, the boy regards him in return. It was always so, he understands, looking at the boy, he would always return to this place. Something rises inside him, a pressure moving through his cells, a sucking, and just as it passes his lips he feels a sharp bite on his finger. His eyes flip open and the sight is recorded in his memory: blood trailing from his hand while before him she suckles a clam to his finger. She looks up at him, those green eyes piercing his own, and he realises that it is dark and the moon is not risen, that he cannot see her, and yet he does.

Fear pulses through his body, a horror at the realisation that she and her clams are eating him, and that he cannot move, and then his fear dissipates in the face of the drifting, in the womb of the lullaby. The world exhales.

Once again he drifts in this warmth, observing memory, and memory observing him back. He sees a cow regarding him from the bush, her newborn calf at her side, and the sound of men approaching. He is deeply afraid, his breath whistling in his throat. They are nearly upon him. Again, the world breathes, that pressure passes out of him and something is birthed, gone from his body. This happens again and again. At times it is horror, sin rising, and at times it is bliss. At each passing and each bite of his hand and bleeding into the water he feels himself dissolving in the beauty of her song. He lies still as she nips at him, ten times, and he bleeds, and humility soaks his soul. At the eleventh reckoning he begins to sob. His little girl is in front of him. He sobs at his hardened heart as she falls into the water, away from him. But this time her face is not one of hate. She is smiling as she ducks under the waves.

He mutters in that bath of bloodied water. Somewhere he is aware that the clams are injecting their seed into the water and that from her flows a milky cloud that envelopes all of them. Somewhere he is aware, also, that one clam has yet to feed.

He lies back, exhausted, unwilling to continue. He feels her take his flesh into her mouth, and he feels the pull of the thorn in his own heart. But he cannot. He is spent.

'Once more,' she whispers within the endless song, 'give me your secrets.'

But he cannot. There is only so much he can part with. And so it circles back out into the ocean, certain to one day wash up again.

He sees her smile, and instead she offers the clam her own finger.

'Thank you.'

Her feet are gone.

He is helped from the tank.

He knows and remembers simultaneously that he is in the lake and she is swirling around him and that whether it is happening now or a thousand years in the future or the past it makes no difference, and then time also is gone.

Sunrise.

The leaves of the tree above become silhouette. He turns. Here is the grave still opened next to him. He rises on this beautiful morning and comes to his knees beside the hole.

The little box is returned.

Gently, he covers it once again.

'Thank you,' he says to the silence of the clearing and the loose soil between his fingers. 'Thank you.'

An alien sound causes him to look up sharply. Uncle Mike turns to the mountain above. There is the sound again, a cry pitching over the cliffs. He knows its meaning. He begins to run.

Quickly he passes from the trees and passes their campsite and the tank in which he cannot see her over the lip, and continues to jog, taking the trail with gripping toes. Again, the cry up there, and now, with the sound he is expecting, the sharp whistle of a man.

He lumbers up the trail, a bear flowing over the ground. He reaches the trailhead and continues, rounding the corner so that the entrance to his valley cannot be seen. And now he waits, the mountain silent and his breath whooshing through his lungs.

The cry again, but no whistle. He squats down, waiting, listening to the footfalls of its approach.

A mountain sheep steps into view, nuzzling the base of the boulder ahead for scattered *wilsner*, relishing the little berries. It has not seen him. He does not want to alarm it. A bleating mountain sheep will alarm its shepherd.

Again the whistle, now from behind the boulder. Uncle Mike does not want to startle the shepherd either. In all his years he has never seen another soul at this lake, but now he realises his assumption was rash. Why would a shepherd not bring his animals to water, especially in a world as uncertain as this? There is no time. He takes up a stone and hides it in his hand.

In a flicker the shepherd appears. He wears a blanket about his shoulders and a balaclava about his face, rolled up to the warm morning. He carries a staff and nonchalantly taps his animal on the flanks, happy to have found it. And then man and beast behold the giant.

'Ha!' the shepherd exclaims, immediately raising his stick. And his sheep is gone, clattering onto a trail only it can see.

'Good morning, brother,' says Uncle Mike, testing a language of the mountain on this man.

'Good morning, brother.'

'I am lost. I was travelling to Mkutweni, the village in these mountains. I come from the Baai. I am thirsty. The weather has been warm.'

The shepherd peers over the shoulder of the strange man before him. Uncle Mike cannot tell whether he knows of the lake or not. The shepherd squats down slowly, carefully, his stick at the ready before him. 'I have come from the Baai. It is the place of the foreigners.'

'How long ago was this, good brother?'

'One week. I took beasts from the farmer Olenof there, and have been driving them to Kweje.'

Abruptly the shepherd pauses, his eyes fixed behind Uncle Mike. He comes to his feet.

Uncle Mike turns also.

She rises before them, striding with grace across the curved rock. She has her eyes to the ground, and then to the humble shepherd. The man bows.

She comes to sit beside Uncle Mike.

'Brother, this is my companion. I am conducting her through these mountains. She knows the Baai also, and is aware of the foreigners there. Tell us, when last did you hear news from that place?'

The shepherd looks everywhere but at the woman before him. He speaks shyly.

'I have heard news not long ago. Many are aware of the foreigners, and many know that one of the people from this land has joined them.'

'Do you mean the men of the *fabrieke*, the owners of the fish houses?'

'No, not them. It is a boy from that place. They say he is a fisherman among fisherman, that he can speak with the fish.'

She listens intently.

'He has led them to a great catch. Even now four of the foreign ships are sailing back to their homeland, heavy with catch, while the fifth is returning to the Baai. It will feed the people. They will send the salted fish to the mines, and even to the city.'

'*Who is this boy?*'

It is she who speaks, and even though she does not use words, the shepherd has heard her. He covers his head with his hands, speaking directly to the rock below him.

'They do not know his face. He wears a mask and he talks to no one. But the people say he is a boy from the back of the Baai.'

'*What are you doing in this part of the mountain? It is far from the trail.*'

The shepherd lies down further, spreading himself on the rock at the sound of her voice in his mind. 'There is good water here. I know a hidden lake.'

The shepherd knows men like the giant, violent men. And he has heard of spirits such as she. He is certain that they mean to eat.

'*I see that you carry your staff. It is for protection and for guiding your sheep?*'

'Yes.'

'*But there is another reason. Your leg is damaged.*'

'Yes. I have damaged my leg falling in these mountains.'

'*May I see to it?*'

She stands. The shepherd raises his eyes to her and the sun behind her. She kneels beside him and helps him sit, taking his injured leg in her hands.

'*There is indeed a lake of good water in these hills. There is a grave there, in the trees. Do you know it?*'

'Yes, I have seen the grave. It is a place of peace. I have camped there with my sheep.'

'*This grave is sacred to me.*'

Heat emanates from her hands. The pain that has been his companion for so long he has almost forgotten it begins to subside. His eyes widen in surprise. And then even more, for she has pierced his eyes with her own. Their green is too bright to behold. He would look away, but he cannot.

'I hear your words. This is a sacred place.'

'*You must avoid that place. I want no one to disturb it.*' She places her hand on his heart. '*My companion and I will leave this place this day. I want you to leave it also and never return. It is my place. It must remain undisturbed.*'

'I will tell no one. That place will remain undisturbed.'

'*Thank you. I wish you a good journey.*'

'Thank you, Great Mother.'

Quickly the shepherd corrals his sheep, and nudging the animal before him he rounds the boulder and is gone, returning to his flock.

She turns to Uncle Mike. '*I am going back to find him. Your pearls are growing and will be everything you hope for.*'

She leans forward and kisses his forehead. And just as the shepherd has become her servant, he knows he has also. He watches her take that same path around the boulder and disappear towards the trail.

He sits, clothed in the silence of the mountain. He would stay at his valley and nurture his dream. But he knows that he cannot. He must follow her, it is fate. He takes a breath, releasing his life past, and then stands. He hurries back down the trail, back to the lake.

The little valley is as he left it. He hurries down, going straight to the tank. He peers inside. It feels as if his heart has disappeared.

The tank is empty. Where each clam lay is an imprint in the sandy bottom. He rushes to the second tank that is still half built. Nothing.

He looks about wildly. The cliffs stare back at him, impassive, as do the trees. He looks to the trail on which he knows she is now walking. He shakes his head, he bangs his fist on the lip of the tank, and then it comes to him. He looks to the lake.

He paces toward it, stepping up to the water's edge where he first laid her within it. He walks until the water covers his knees and then his thighs, and then he sees. A clam at rest on the bottom, its greedy mouth open to the sun. He squats down into the water and reaches his hand out, stroking the lip of the creature. It does not close. He places his finger gently on the flesh of the mantle within, and still the mouth stays open.

He looks beyond this clam and spies more. Here are the twelve. All with their mouths open, all eating the sun.

He is about to stand, drawing his hand back, when a further vision grabs him. Against the white of his hand something is see-sawing, a multitude. Carefully he raises his hand to the surface, cupping his other hand next to it, bringing these see-sawing creatures nearer his eye. He places his nose to the water, his eye near to the veil, and spies them. They are the veliger, the young clams.

Uncle Mike releases them.

He dips his mouth into the water and immediately he tastes it: salt. He looks to the cliffs, and the trees, and the cascading waterfall, and all return his gaze.

'*Grow*,' he whispers to all the creatures in this valley, to all his new clams, and then he walks out of the water. With urgency he takes all that he dragged over this mountain and sinks it into the lake. All of his implements and tanks and preparations are washed away.

Finally he stands with nothing but the clothes on his body, and then he turns from the lake and jogs up the trail. He does not go into the trees. He has already begged his leave. And besides, this place is his heart, and he takes it with him.

CHAPTER FOURTEEN

Much has changed in the Baai. The town is abuzz with the news that a new captain has joined the foreign fleet, a man that can fish like no other, and that he has led them to a spectacular catch. 'He can speak with fish,' is the refrain whispering through the sorting halls of the six remaining *fabrieke*. 'He is the boy of the Morkel *fabriek*, the one with the broken lip. He has joined with them.'

'Where did Yoguchi find him?' the six mutter among themselves – Van Deventer, Mostert, Weatherall-Thomas, the Schaafsma brothers and Mocke – as they speed the main road with their hand phones pasted to their windshields and their worries filling their double cabs.

'The catch is a big one.'

'It is over a thousand ton.'

'Never has a catch in the Baai been that big.'

'Will Yoguchi share it with us?'

'He must!'

The men know that one of Yoguchi's five vessels is trawling back to them, riding low in the water. And they know that the four others have peeled away in the open ocean and have long since crossed into international seas.

'Of course he will. What else will he do with such a multitude?'

The men fret and hurry and prepare their sorting halls, opening the rooms that have gathered nothing but dust these seven long years. Only old Mocke drives easy, alone in his Datsun; only he does not feed the worry. Instead, he looks out his windshield at the building cloud and marks the coming of autumn.

And while the six call to each other through their phones, the rest whisper. The town knows. The wallowing trawler has been spotted out in the deep by little craft who have raced ahead of it, spreading the message. The strident calls via two-way radio that echo from onshore receivers are a signal to all. The airwaves twist with fish, fish that must be processed before they rot. All along the coast men and women return to their *fabrieke*. The factory doors are opened, the boilers are lit, and they wait.

Many forsake their place at the line, instead streaming to the harbour in the hopes of seeing what is said to be true, that the ships of the Yamamoto fleet can freeze a fish and then bring it gasping back from the dead. They fill the quay and they wait as the fifth vessel rounds the breakwater wall. The *Fugisha* eases into dock, its hold aligning with the old loading pipe waiting to receive the catch.

Uncle Mike moves among the crowd. He has dressed himself in the clothing of the men from the Baai. He wears the denim shorts and pocketed shirt, the shade hat perched on his head and knife and hand phone clipped to his belt, but he is not one of them any longer.

The throng think nothing of him, they know Mike Morkel and his *fabriek*, but the six are quick to mark him.

'*Middag, Oom* – afternoon, Uncle,' says Uncle Mike as he slips in beside old Mocke, looming two heads taller than the little man.

'Mikey,' nods Mocke, not taking his eyes from the docking trawler. 'So, you are back.'

All observe Yoguchi moving along the deck, clothed as always in his light jeans and running shoes, dark shades and laundered open-necked shirt. All watch as he skips across the great ship towering above them and the best of their boats, even though the *Fugisha* is the smallest of the Yamamoto fleet. Yoguchi looks out to the gathered crowd and raises a hand above his smile.

'Hello!' He hops to the lowered ladder and comes dancing down to the quay. 'We are glad you could all join us!'

Beneath Yoguchi the portside loading hatch is sliding open.

'We are about to show you all something special! We are lucky we could find a decent pipe.'

Yoguchi points beyond the crowd. All turn to see the Baai's old harbour hand, Mr Reagan Monroe, pulling the big loading pipe on its retractable bracket near. As wide as a tractor tyre, the nozzle will latch to the hatch and suck the harvest from the vessel. From there the catch will be pumped along the length of the quay to the waiting lorries.

Uncle Mike turns to look at them, making use of his vantage point over the crowd. Seven lorries are lined up there, his own man Salie at the wheel of one. Uncle Mike nods to himself. He has not yet spoken to Salie, but the man knows his mind.

'Wait!'

It is Yoguchi calling as he ducks under the suspended hose to put a hand on Monroe's shoulder. He speaks with the old harbour hand as the hatch slides fully open, revealing the frozen catch within.

The crowd edge closer, eager to see.

Monroe stands aside, swinging the hose on its suspended bracket away. Yoguchi comes to stand in front of the hatch, jumping up onto a big mooring cleat to better face the crowd. His new height puts him at eye level with Uncle Mike. The little man flashes a smile to him only, before turning to those gathered.

'People of the Baai,' he calls to them. 'Our ships have hunted and we have come home victorious. We have brought you a good catch, and we hope you will enjoy it as our gesture of friendship.'

The people of the Baai cheer.

Yoguchi points across the crowd to Uncle Mike and the gathered six.

'Your factories are ready to work, and we have brought fish for you to work. So, work we must! Process this catch, and then let us celebrate.'

Yoguchi steps aside to reveal the open hold.

It is a gloomy hole inside which dark bodies and white ice can just be seen.

'Mr Monroe, would you mind showing us one of our frozen fish?'

Monroe starts, surprised at the request.

'Come on, sir. Simply reach in to our hold and bring out one of our fish. I'm sure all would like to see it.'

Monroe shrugs and smiles. It is not a tough task and it feels good to have the eyes of the crowd on him. He steps forward, hesitantly reaching into the dark.

'Take any,' calls Yoguchi, 'bring it out. Let us see!'

Monroe does so, bringing not one but two *tunny* out into the light, each frozen to the other, their eyes icy mirrors.

'Pass them round!'

Monroe does so.

'And another!' calls Yoguchi, infected by the excitement of all of them.

Monroe passes another and then another out from the bursting hold. All know the feel of fish, all know the feel of ice, and all know the sight of death. These fish are fresh-caught and frozen, just like any other catch brought forth from the deep sea. They are as frozen as any fish any Baaier has ever seen.

Yoguchi watches as the crowd pass them from palm to palm, a wide smile upon his face. He turns to look up to the deck to one of his men there. He nods, and the man in turn looks up to the bridge, and nods also.

'Watch the hold!' calls Yoguchi, and all eyes turn to the portal. There is a moment while all are waiting, and then there is a hiss within the hold.

Again there is a pause, and then all rear back as a scent of lavender washes over them, and then they cry out. Because the frozen hold begins to seethe. Thousands of fish are wriggling, bodies slipping from the open hatch and falling to the water where the crowd surge to watch them hit the green and dart away, alive.

'Aahh!'

'They live!'

'Monroe, quickly!'

The hose swings in to cover the hatch and catch those fish wriggling back to the water. The old machine turns over and the hose judders to life, roaring and shaking as the multitude begin to stream down the pipe that snakes above their heads toward the distant lorries. The diesel engine roars as the river of life is sucked along, and the pipe belches as fish begin to spew into the load bed of the first lorry. With all eyes on the trucks none are watching the ship, none but Uncle Mike, who has not taken his eyes from the little man. He watches as Yoguchi looks to the sailor on the deck, who looks to the bridge. On that cue the door there opens and from it steps another man. He is dressed in the robes of these foreigners, wound across his body and up about his face. A headdress rests on his head, clearly the mark of the captain. The strange figure stands there a moment, and by osmosis the crowd notice him. All swing their attention back to the ship and to the man towering over them all.

'It's the boy from the Morkel *fabriek*,' whispers one. 'It's our own fisher.'

He is indeed the size of Jono the fisher, and he is indeed the shape of Jono the fisher. He stands forlorn like the boy always did, and then, before their eyes, he straightens. All mark it: it is the movement of boy to man, from lost to found. All see it, all feel it, all know it to be that forlorn boy having found his home.

'Jono!' shouts one among them. 'Take your mask off, let us see you!'

The figure moves, his right arm sweeping up to cross his chest, and then suddenly he freezes, and his head turns sharply. None understand the strange gesture, and there is a deepening silence until, with a sudden flourish, the strange captain turns this oddity into a bow. The crowd laugh. Here is Jono, their boy, covered in the stuffy robes of the foreigners but still with the love of laughing of any man or woman of the Baai. They giggle at his antics. Even Yoguchi is smiling.

'Hey, Jono! Don't forget your manners! Just because you a captain now, don't mean you not a Baaier!'

'Jono! Show us your pretty face!'

The crowd laugh louder, full of the hope of the catch. The captain spreads his arms, asking for quiet. He pauses, holding them all in his thrall, and then he salutes them. His message is clear: 'All will be well.' And the crowd burst into a cheer. One of their own is within this strange ship, one of their own.

He turns and disappears inside.

'Good on you, Jono!'

'Cap-tain! Cap-tain! Cap-tain!'

Uncle Mike turns to Yoguchi and catches the man staring directly back at him. Yoguchi holds his gaze for a moment, and then he too turns, and is gone.

Behind Uncle Mike the harbour hand Monroe has joined the six and is handing out paper chits.

'We will record your catch on the weigh bridge,' Monroe is informing them while pressing six chits into six waiting hands. 'Mr Yoguchi is offering you last season's price on *tunny*. He is sure you will agree.'

The men do agree, each fingering the paper before them, each immersed in their own calculations. How do you quantify the rain when finally it falls on the desert?

'Uncle Mike,' states Monroe, pressing a seventh sales chit into the big man's paw. 'Payment terms are one week from today.'

The crowd is dispersing and the six are moving off to the trucks, where one by one the hose is depositing a shower of wriggling tunny into each flatbed. Two have already clattered to life and rolled out of the harbour.

Uncle Mike remains on the clearing quay. He touches his chin as his eyes turn to the metal trawler. The hull of the ship is still riding low, despite the amount of catch already offloaded. He imagines the weight that must remain within, building a picture for himself of the mass of fish this ship can contain. And then he does what his brain is aching to do: he multiplies that wonderful number by four. In his mind's eye he sees the other ships steaming even now toward the foreigners' homeland, each with fourteen of the Baai's lorry loads tucked into their holds. He taps his grizzled finger to his chin. He knows now more than ever that it is crumbs only that are reserved for the men and women of this place. Finally he turns, and he too leaves the emptying quay.

Throughout the day, the lines in the *fabrieke* churn through the load that has been shared among the seven. The sorting halls tumble with activity.

And while the *fabrieke* smoke and clatter, so the older people descend on the old fairgrounds of the harbour. There they lay open the pits that have been filled in with rubble these seven years, and they hang coloured paper in streamers, and they unfold tables to be topped with the breads, salads, puddings and baskets of meat that each *fabriek* will provide as per their share, as was done in days before.

'The drought is over!' is the refrain that runs through the laying of every branch of wood in the fire pits, and every plate on the table, and every line of streamers drifting in the fresh wind. Autumn is blessing the Baai with the last days of summer, and tonight the seven will host the celebration.

But while the new harvest is chopped and sliced through the lines in six factories, at one of them a load of fish lies untouched. At the Morkel *fabriek* the workers stand idle around the truck while Salie talks with Uncle Mike in his office, and while Boysen, Salie's oldest, leans by the lorry cab with a cigarette at his lip to ensure the stinking fish are untouched.

At length Salie emerges, hurrying, unhappy, a box cradled in his arms.

'Move, move,' he gestures to Boysen so that the man jumps away and Salie dumps the box on the passenger seat, the door hanging open at the hinge.

'Now come around,' he calls, fishing into the box with one hand and extracting a brown envelope. He holds it aloft, evidence to the gathering that he is empowered to speak.

'There is no work today.'

Glances ripple through the gathering, and mutters.

'What you mean?'

'No work, Mr Janse. Today we do not process. But don't worry. Uncle Mike has his *mense*, his people, at heart. We will all be paid. Full wages.'

He waves the brown envelope above their heads.

'Everyone. Paid for not a stitch of work. It's the lucky day of you's lazy bastards.'

Salie tilts the envelope above him to see the name scrawled by hand across the cover: 'Denis January.'

A hand is raised in the sea of heads, and there is a ripple as Mr January sidles his way to the cab.

'There's your packet.'

Salie hands Mr January his brown envelope.

'Sophie Richards.'

And Salie places the next in the hands of Sophie Richards, woman of the line of the Morkel *fabriek*.

'Uncle Mike says not to worry, you's lazy *varke*. Come to the party tonight. He will see you's there. Celebrate! Fish are back in the Baai.'

The night draws in and the people of the Baai begin to gather. They have worked for twenty-four hours, sleeping next to the line when knives began to slip from weariness, and then they stood to continue when the cacophony of a full sorting floor woke them. And now they have hoisted themselves, and returned home, and bathed, and they arrive at the harbour grounds with a box of wine already inside, ready to celebrate.

The fires crackle high and above them the stars burn. The town is thronged around the fire pits. And then, streaming out of the darkness, comes a beast. It tears through the spark-filled air, floating sinuous above the flames, eyes flashing from a painted face. The fisher folk stare and point as the dragon floats above them, its head darting beneath and then above its flowing tail. Under the beast Yoguchi's men move in unison. The beat of a drum holds the dragon high until suddenly the pounding stops and in the silence the creature falls to the fires.

Yoguchi's men step aside as the dragon is consumed. All observe in silence as the creation dies and once again there is but flame, and smoke, and man. All are riveted, but one.

She is at their edges. She moves through them without sound. She, who is here to find her love. She knows he is here. She has come far, outrunning the bear as he chased her all along the trail, and avoiding all eyes as she observed the docking of the ship with the rest, and saw the captain revealed above the crowd.

'*My love*,' she had spoken in the way that only he is able to hear. And he had heard. His head had come up sharply to spy her in her hiding place in the girders of the selling deck, looking down upon them all.

He had raised his hand to her, before once again turning to the crowd, his people. And she had thrilled to it. And now he is here and waiting for her, and together they will escape.

As Yoguchi's men stand uncertainly in the aftermath of their dragon dance, peering at the gaily lit throng around them, and a banjo picks up a new tune and one by one they are taken by the hand and given food and drink and friendship, she drifts on their periphery, following the trail of her love.

Yoguchi stands near the flames, his cigarette to his smile.

A ripple in the crowd causes him to turn. Here come the consortium: Van Deventer, Mostert, Weatherall-Thomas, the Schaafsma brothers and old Mocke. Mike Morkel is not among them.

'Mr Yoguchi,' coughs the big Van Deventer, sticking out his hand. 'We congratulate you on good fishing.'

'Mr Van Deventer, thank you,' replies Yoguchi, stepping forward with his own hand outstretched.

'We thank you also for diverting your catch to our processing plants. We were pleased to work it, to our fashion.'

'I thought it proper,' says Yoguchi, stepping nearer and raising a hand to Van Deventer's shoulder. 'These are your seas after all; I am but a guest here.'

Van Deventer's eyes flicker to Mocke before he continues: 'We have come to settle with you.'

The men behind Van Deventer shuffle, revealing a brown envelope clutched in each hand. All their faces are drawn in the same relief: that of surrender.

'That is very generous,' remarks Yoguchi, his open arms drawing the group closer to his circle. 'But let us discuss. I feel that you are too kind. Perhaps we can sit somewhere with a plate of food and talk things through? Tonight is after all for celebration.'

Easily Yoguchi shepherds the men to where a table with eight places has been set.

'I see Uncle Mike has not accompanied you.'

'He will be here, I am sure of it,' replies Van Deventer. 'His workers are here. He will come. There is no sense in staying away.'

'No,' replies Yoguchi, 'there is not.'

He raises his eyes to the stars and listens amid the cacophony for something.

Blue smoke from the fires drifts among the trees. And she glides beneath them. Here, on the far edge of the harbour grounds, at the place where fishers can walk the open path skirting the ground straight to the quays and the boats shifting at their mooring lines, the foreign fishers have raised their camp. These men of the sea have been on their vessels or confined to their tents for all the months since arriving at the Baai, these tents are their separate home where, until tonight, no man or woman of the Baai has ventured. Tonight, on the gift of their shared catch, that will change. Tonight a new generation will be made.

But she is not concerned with their futures – she is headed for her own. There is one among all that she can hear. '*My love*' she hears him call. And she answers: '*My love.*'

The tents rise up around her, rows of bunk shelters for the fishers, a canvas hall thrown up around tables for eating and television, a place of exercise for these strange men, and a canvas home for Yoguchi, where he speaks with headquarters. She passes all of this, drawn to the water and the open sea that laps against the ocean side of the breaker wall. His call draws her there, and she is not surprised. Of course he will be at the water. What will he say when he sees her walking? What will she say, to see his new authority draped around him? How has he changed, and she? What will have changed between them and what will be the same? She wonders all of this with delight and desire, as she leaves the tents and the noise of the celebration behind.

Here is the whoosh of breakers sighing through rock and the fresh wind of the ocean. Here is the possibility of the night.

'*My love.*'

The silhouette of the *dolosse*, the giant concrete T-shaped moulds of the breakwater, are ahead of her. The stark shapes move apart suddenly. A shadow separates itself from their concrete outlines: a being with a head-dress that peaks toward the sky.

He turns to her.

There is open ground ahead and she pauses, remaining in the last cover of the tangle of bush, afraid to cross the last barrier between them.

'*Why did you leave, my love?*'

The being raises its hand to her – his hand.

'*My love.*'

He raises his other.

'*My love.*'

Her lip trembles, all of the pain of the past weeks rising in her body. All that she has seen, all the distance she has travelled, all the confusion, and all the longing for him. '*Where did you go?*'

He makes to move towards her, and she can no longer stay away. She steps forward, shrouded in white, standing on her new legs.

'*I have come to you. I have come to the land for you.*'

The figure does not move, his peak silhouetted against the stars.

'*My love.*'

She takes another careful pace forward, stepping into the last of the awful gulf of their separation.

'*My love?*'

Suddenly an explosion of white light. Her world is devastated by it, her pupils seared. She lifts her hands to her eyes at the same time as a rush of figures come swarming out of the dark.

'*My love!*'

She strikes out, attempting to turn and run, but she is hooked by innumerable hands that drag her to the dirt.

'My love!' she shouts from her own throat, a strange shriek, her strength coming to her as she strikes out at these figures, raking them, hearing the grunt of one of them as he falls, but then a new explosion. The world wobbles as something is bashed into her skull. She falls, her eyes on him, and sees that he is overwhelmed also. They are everywhere, men in dark garb with their heads shrouded.

She shrieks but these creatures do not stop.

She calls and he cannot help her.

The fight drains from her body.

She relents, dropping her head to the dirt. Up there the stars shimmer; among them the scorpion beams.

'*And what is this?*'

The words are formed in a strange tongue. The voice is soft and strident, as light as a drip of poison. She will not forget the sound of it. It is the first moment of the rest of her life. She looks up, and for the first time sees the scorpion curled in the sky. A face appears, blotting out the creature. It smiles, a coal glowing at the lips before swirling away in smoke.

Yoguchi peers down at her.

'*And what are you?*' he repeats, shocking her with his voice vibrating not in the world, but in her own mind. He speaks as she does.

He regards her, dark eye to green. '*What a wonderful creature,*' he croons, as a drugged cloth is clamped over her nose, and she spins away into the dark.

Fragrant smoke drifts from a brazier up into the high reaches of Yoguchi's tent. Up there the night's breeze swirls, pulling the smoke away. His quarters are functional. On the far wall is a CB radio station where he confers nightly with home. Filing cabinets are stacked next to it, tracking around the back of the tent. In the middle of the room is a table on which he dines, and where he reads, and here on the nearside is his camp cot, and his indulgence: an Audio-Technica turntable. It sits on a low table beside the cot; a set of headphones is placed on top of its closed lid and a long cable stretches easily to his pillow. But now is not the time for him to lie and dream within the world of his music, because his cot is occupied. She lies naked on it, asleep.

Yoguchi stands near the ashtray, his cigarette forgotten as he studies the creature and looks upon his own future. She is very nearly seven feet tall, and she is exquisite. She is woman and she is fish. Her body is moulded by water, every joint and sinew blending to the flow of liquid, smoothed and powerful. She radiates power. He leans closer, finding the path of muscle from thigh to belly that remembers a mighty tail. He finds webbing between her fingers, and he finds the twin slits in her neck, frilled with gill. He runs his fingers across her without touching, drinking her with his eyes, marvelling. She is fish, and yet her body calls to him. Her jewel-shaped eyes and high cheekbones are haunting. Her hips make him ache, the pale slit between her legs, dusted pink at its edges, puts fire in his blood. She is a rendering of high geometry. He longs to see her swim.

He puts his hand out to her, pausing before his fingers touch the sacred flesh. He breathes, aware of this moment of his own existence, this peeling apart of the veil between himself and his destiny. She is a creature the likes of which he has never seen, and he is certain she was created only for him. Lightly he takes her fingers. He closes his eyes and trains his mind to hers.

He is not prepared for the onslaught. Within her is the deepest ocean, howling with all of its multitudinous life. He hears the pulse of every being swimming out there, a great host churning in an avalanche of sound.

'*Eat!*' roars through his ears, flesh, bones, and he snatches his hand away and falls to the ground, his hand on his wildly beating heart. He stares at this creature, wide-eyed as she looks at him.

Before she can say a word there is a scratching at the tent flap.

'Come,' orders Yoguchi, standing quickly.

A sailor enters, his eyes carefully finding his master's and then holding them rather than looking about the room, rather than meeting the green eyes of the creature.

'There is a problem outside. It is the *kyojin* – the giant.'

Yoguchi glances back at her.

'Tie her, and bring her, and keep ten men on her at all times.'

Yoguchi hurries through the fresh night with his men behind him. His face is painted with intent. The bear has come to play, and he is grateful. If he can catch it, it will buy him years of favour. Unbidden, a pair of green eyes rise in his mind. He is still vibrating with her, full of the roar of that multitude. He shakes his head. He must focus. 'One fish at a time, Yoguchi,' he murmurs to himself. 'First we catch our sailfish, and then we hunt our whale.'

A voice rings out in the distance: 'Yo-guuuu-chi!'

It emanates from the fire pits ahead. Yoguchi, man of the rank of first captain of the Yamamoto corporation, admiral of the southern fleet, permits himself a smile. The bear is bellowing, already full of anger. This is precisely the kind of bear that will walk into a trap.

He notes that the music has ceased and a brilliant orange light strafes through the drifting smoke.

'YO-GUUUU-CHI!'

Once again the bear roars.

'Bring the creature near, but keep her gagged and hidden,' he orders the man who hurries at his side. 'She must not escape.'

The man nods and peels back among the men following.

Yoguchi reaches the fringes of the crowd and makes his way among them. All are turned in the direction of the fire pits, where just beyond them one of the Morkel *fabriek* trucks has pulled up, its powerful headlights cutting the smoke with fluorescent beams. A stench emanates from the lorry, the smell of rotting fish. From on top of the cab an orange searchlight plays across them all, guided by a massive hand.

'Yoguchi!'

Uncle Mike is standing astride the cab of his truck, the spotlight in one hand and a loudhailer in the other. 'Show yourself!'

Yoguchi steps into the open, his eyes cast up to the big man.

'Mr Morkel!'

Uncle Mike turns and finds the man in his light. He flicks it left and right and finds the six also. Already they have the faces of strangers.

'Uncle Mike,' says Yoguchi, stepping forward with conciliation in his tone. 'Come down. Our table for eight is set. We have been waiting for you.' He raises a hand to shield his eyes. 'Would you lower your light? I cannot see you.'

'Mikey,' speaks Van Deventer, '*kom nou* – come now.' He walks forwards, wanting to speak quietly, wanting to get this man out of the eyes of all of them. 'There is place for all of us here.'

'Where are the other four trawlers, Yoguchi?'

'I have sent them home, you know this. The catch is frozen, they will feed my people.'

'And *my* people?'

'Your people are not so many, Mr Morkel. One load for you is enough.'

'One fish of ours for you is too much!'

Uncle Mike looks among the crowd and sees the face of old Mocke. 'You will let this man take our fish? We offered him the chance to work with us, and instead he will work over us. He was not born here; this is not his Baai.'

'You were not born here either, Mikey.'

'The table is laid for eight,' calls Yoguchi. 'There is no leader at our table. All of us are equal. Come down and speak with us.'

'We are not equal to your ships.'

Uncle Mike turns to the crowd. 'These men have come here because their own fish are gone. They have built their ships to sail the world in search of new fishing grounds, because their own have been decimated. It is these men that have taken the fish from our ocean. Was it us? Did we fish so much?' He turns to look at Yoguchi. 'They will leave when they have taken all they can, and we will have nothing.'

'We already had nothing,' shouts a man of the Baai. 'The *fabrieke* were closed. Now today, we had work.'

'For how long will you have it? This catch is caught in the deep ocean where we cannot go, this catch is many times the size we have ever harvested. How long will the fish remain?'

Uncle Mike lowers his light so that all can see his face. The big man is weary. 'I do not come from here. I come from the mountains. My people were like you. We worked the land and hunted and required little. And then outsiders came, and with them war, and nothing remained. You people were spared the war, but you know of it.'

He raises his finger and trains it to the foreign vessel at mooring in the harbour. 'We do not know it now, but if we let these men stay then the time will come when we realise that we have lost everything. What do we know of these people? Nothing!'

The eyes and faces that stare up to Uncle Mike in the white of the headlights and the soft orange of the distant harbour flood lights and the bright blues and reds and yellows of the festive lights strung about the overhanging trees digest the big man's words. There is truth in what he says, but also, today there was work.

Yoguchi says nothing. He can see his trap uncoiling itself to settle around the big man's neck. He climbs onto a nearby table, carefully placing his sneakered feet between the food plates, and raises himself above the crowd.

'Uncle Mike,' he calls, and all the assembled eyes turn to him. 'You speak truth. I cannot fault you.' As Yoguchi speaks so one of his sailors begins to translate to his men, a strange echo ringing out across the crowd. 'You speak of losing your home. I can sympathise. That war touched all of us; it touched my people too.' And Yoguchi points to his sailors who are dotted throughout the crowd, many of them already with a person of the Baai at their side. 'Just as you find yourself in this Baai, far from your home and those you once loved, so my people wander the seas. Like you, we are forced to roam. Unlike you, we have not yet found a new home.'

Yoguchi pauses now, and retrieves his packet of cigarettes from his shirt pocket. Gently he pulls one from the pack, and to many it seems, with pain in his movements. They can see the weight of the years on him also, and the years of service to his people. He is not so different to Uncle Mike.

Yoguchi strikes his lighter and bends to touch his cigarette to flame. He coughs once, and the people mark it. 'You speak of domination from us, but you seem to forget that we have shown you only the opposite.' He points to Uncle Mike. 'We have provided catch for all to work, we have made favourable terms with the *fabrieke*, and we have done even more than that.'

He looks around at the crowd. He allows the silence to expand. He clasps his hands before him, and then spreads them into the air. 'We have engaged one of your own and made him our captain. What could be a greater symbol of our intent than choosing one of you to lead us?'

There is a disturbance near the tents. A ripple passes through the crowd as all turn to it. The captain seen on the boat is there, his headdress rising above them and his robes wrapped across his body. At Yoguchi's bidding he is helped up onto a table.

'Here stands our captain, Jono of the Baai. A fisher with such talent that he outmatches all of us. A fisher, Uncle Mike, from your very own *fabriek*. Here stands the very symbol of our partnership. Just as our ships bring technology from which you can learn, so we have discovered a fisher among you with such talent that we must make him our commander. As you all know, it was your boy Jono that led us to the harvest that we celebrate today.'

The crowd watch as Jono's cart, the one that all saw him pull daily along the boiling tar and the rain-lashed tar and the cold winter tar while dressed in his rags, is held up by two of Yoguchi's sailors. Every one of the Baai's people knows that cart.

'People of the Baai,' Yoguchi calls, pointing to the robed captain. 'You all know your Jono, who spent his days toiling for the Morkel *fabriek*. Tell us, Uncle Mike, what did you do for this boy, apart from condemn him to live alone in a hovel?'

Uncle Mike blinks. He had not anticipated the man's question, even though now, once it is uttered, it is the most obvious question of all. In a flash he sees the trap laid for him, he sees the noose drifting down.

The eyes of the crowd turn to him, eyes that each share the burden of guilt that all are so eager to part with.

'I gave him everything he needed.'

'Everything? You gave him a hovel, a little fishing boat, and a berth at miserly pay. You would not even provide him with petrol. He was the beggar of this Baai, forced to row while others used engines, and yet he is the greatest fisher of all of us.'

The figure of the captain stands without moving, staring steadfastly at Uncle Mike.

'I gave him what he asked for. He never asked for more.'

'Never?' Heads turn from Yoguchi to Uncle Mike, and back again. 'I watched him corral the biggest blue sailfish yet caught in the Baai so that the men of the Baai might broker a deal with me. And I watched him do it despite an injury delivered by your own hand. Was that not his way of asking, his way of showing loyalty?'

'I gave him what he deserved.'

'What he deserved? You broke him. You worked him into the dust. Why? Because of his crippled mouth?'

At the fringe of the crowd there is a new movement, unseen by all but those standing up high. Uncle Mike, Yoguchi and the captain can see a figure there. The sailors are struggling with it, and then she is revealed, tied securely. She raises her eyes to Uncle Mike and they pierce him, even in the dark, even from that distance.

'Why do you hate this boy? Is it because of his race?'

A delicious gasp from the crowd.

'The boy is not like you. He is the son of an outsider to this Baai, just like you. Is that why you hate him?'

The crowd turn to Uncle Mike, and sentiment turns also. The pack want blood. Uncle Mike's guilt is their guilt also, and they cannot stand it.

'Do you hate him because of his race or is there a deeper reason? Who is this boy?' asks Yoguchi, pointing to the masked captain. 'Do the good people of the Baai know the tale that you have tried so hard to keep silent, but can keep silent no more?'

Uncle Mike does not speak. He knows the truth has come home to roost. Instead, he looks to her.

'*I am sorry*,' he says, now knowing that his journey with her will be short, not knowing if she will hear.

'Do they know how you imprisoned this boy and left him to the care of your man Salie as nothing more than a cow or a pig? Do they know how you caught him in debt, how you withheld even gasoline from him so that he could not use his motor and it was impossible for him to fill his daily quota? Do they know how you paralysed this boy's ability to fish, and then accused him of laziness?'

Uncle Mike searches the crowd. He sees Salie out there, he sees Mocke out there, these the only ones that know his intimate life. And then he cannot help himself. Once again, he looks to her.

'*What are you sorry for?*' she asks, her eyes boring into his soul.

'Do they know of how you beat this boy week in and week out, how you broke him year after year in punishment?'

The crowd mutter their agreement.

'Many of you remember Uncle Mike's beautiful daughter. Her name was Margaret.'

At the sound of her name Uncle Mike finds strength. His voice booms out, demanding silence. 'Enough!'

'Oh!' Yoguchi is quick to maintain his advantage. 'Now you speak?'

'You do not speak of her!'

But the crowd will speak of her. They turn to Yoguchi, their silence permission to continue.

'Not many know that at one time Margaret was to marry a boy of the choosing of her father.' He points to Van Deventer, who nods his assent. 'The son of Van Deventer was to be her betrothed, and the Morkel and Van Deventer *fabrieke* were to merge. But the spirited girl refused. Why?' Yoguchi turns his face to Uncle Mike, and the crowd follow. 'Because she had already found her love. And who was he? He was the son of poor fisherfolk, refugees like Uncle Mike himself, trying to make a new life in the Baai. He was a nobody. A man who had no pedigree but his heart, as we all do.'

There is nodding among the crowd, there is remembering. That young fisher was known, that shy boy of the shy folk that arrived in the Baai some twenty years before, that boy with the broken lip.

'You refused your daughter Margaret the right to marry the man she loved. You drove them to run from you, and like the unbending man that you are, you chased them.'

All eyes are riveted to the face of Uncle Mike. The truth of Yoguchi's words is written there, playing across his features like fire in the dry summer fields.

'*What are you sorry for?*'

Uncle Mike sees her green eyes. He cannot answer her.

'They ran and hid from your violent temper, and you chased them when you heard of their hiding place out on the northern coast. You hunted them and they fled to the sea, and you chased them still.'

Uncle Mike finds the face of Salie in the crowd. There is only one man who knows this aspect of the tale, only one who was with him on that day.

'You chased them in your own vessel and cornered them, those gentle two. That shy fisherman who did nothing but attempt to provide for his love. You hurt him, did you not? You, the great and powerful Uncle Mike. You struck him and he fell to the water, attempting to defend his love, did you not?'

'*I am sorry.*'

Her green eyes watch him.

'And after her love fell into the water you attempted to restrain your daughter, did you not, ordering her to return to you even when her love was drowning. And then she spat on you, did she not? And flung herself into the waves.'

Silence rings out across the harbour picnic grounds.

'It was you who caused your own daughter to be lost, along with the husband she chose, and you, who in your grief, could not relinquish your own hate. For there was another with them.'

A log in the fire pit snaps with a crack, and against the breakwater the distant surf booms. Yoguchi waits, allowing the fullness of the night to witness his following words.

'There was a child,' he says finally.

By his face, all know it to be true. Their eyes move to the figure of the captain.

For one final time Uncle Mike looks to her, but she is gone.

Yoguchi gestures to the masked captain who stands silent, watching them all with his cart beside him. 'Uncle Mike. You accuse me of coming here to defile your home, when it is you that has defiled your own blood. Jono, the greatest fisher in the Baai, perhaps the greatest in the world, and your own grandson.' He pauses, and then: 'The great Uncle Mike! He who murdered his own blood.'

Uncle Mike roars. He smashes the console beside him. The hydraulics of the truck begin to churn, the load of rotting fish he has refused to process sliding in a slimy mess towards the fires as he launches himself into the air. His rage is set free. Below him the faces of the people of the Baai gape at him, these he has sworn to protect. Salie, he who let loose his secret. Mocke and the six, who could have created a free Baai with him, if only they had courage. The boy, who even now harries and pricks at him, after all these twenty years. Uncle Mike's jump is impossible. He flies above the crowd, his massive body propelled by equally massive power, his diamond eyes pinpointed on his prize.

Yoguchi is grinning at him, full of the glee of his public unmasking of the last free man of the Baai, until his smile turns to terror. For Uncle Mike is heading straight for him. He shrieks.

Uncle Mike smashes into the table on which Yoguchi stands. 'You!' He roars, grabbing a foot and then a knee and then the hip of the frantic foreigner. 'You would kill us all!' He flails for the neck of the man in a bid to snap it, howling as he feels the bone of an arm splinter under his fingers. But Yoguchi's sailors are loyal and they come rushing to his aid.

'Coward!' screams Uncle Mike as he is pulled down by their avalanche. Blades begin to pierce him. His meaty hands move from Yoguchi who is slipping from his grasp and find the necks of the sailors around him. He roils with them, laying furious waste as their knives pierce him over and over, and even the masked captain is dragged down into the melee, his headdress falling to the dirt amid the fighting sailors.

'Fight!' roars Uncle Mike, desperate to look into Yoguchi's accursed eyes before he dashes the light out of them. But the man is quick, dancing out of reach as the blades fall and darkness and blood begin to crowd Uncle Mike's vision.

'You will die for your sins,' shouts Uncle Mike under the weight of them, trying to reach that dancing wraith. But his strength is leaking away and finally he subsides. It is chaos as his body is dragged across the stones, and darkness as their knives continue to rain down.

'*Do you hear me?*' he hears whispered in his mind, her voice like wind chimes.

'*I do,*' he replies, and in the dark he sees her eyes. '*I am dying.*'

'*No, not yet.*'

'*I tried to set him free. Don't you see?*'

In this twilit world he sees her hand rise up. The barb of the cephalopod is held between her fingers.

'*It was not enough.*'

He feels her finger whisper upon his arm, crawling to the place where the boy stabbed him, now reopened by Yoguchi's sailors.

'*Can you see me?*'

'*I can.*'

And once again her face changes to the mask his daughter wore before she fell to the waves, and once again he feels the breaking of that piece of his heart.

'*Burn,*' she whispers as the gland touches the wound and the poison's fire bursts through his cells. '*Burn like those you have caused to burn.*'

And he burns.

Later that night, when the people of the Baai have returned home, each carrying a parcel of food, and the harbour grounds have been cleared and the fires extinguished, when the sailors of Yamamoto lie in their cots and Yoguchi murmurs into his radio, his splintered arm held to his side, Uncle Mike lies on a table in the canteen of the tent village. His body is pierced fifty-seven times and his blood is soaked into the ground beneath him.

About him are those he has slain. To his right are seven men on seven tables. Five are foreign sailors and two are men of the Baai. Their features have smoothed. In death the foreigners and the men of the Baai have merged. All are meat, awaiting the hungry soil.

To his left lies another: the captain. The headdress is gone and the mask is pulled aside. The neck is crushed, a deep bruising beneath the skin, and a line of blood meanders from the nostril. The features of the captain are fine: the features of a boy, a young dreamer, one who can hear what others cannot. The jaw is covered by a sparse beard, barely enough to conceal the cleft in the lip beneath, and the hair is wispy and flutters in the night's breeze. The eyes are open, looking sightlessly to the canvas above, and they are blue. They are not the dark eyes of Jono, but those of a boy from another place; a boy with a similar gift, caught in the lives of others.

In the canteen of the foreign fishers all is stillness among the corpses that lie there. All but one. For the big man breathes, so softly it is impossible to see or hear. And his heart beats, so gently it is impossible to measure. And his mind howls, so finely that none can hear it but her as she lies bound and gagged in the gently rocking hold of the *Fugisha*.

'*Burn*,' she whispers to him. And he does.

PART III

CHAPTER FIFTEEN

The coastline north of the Baai is wild and empty. Here the vast farms of the *innelanders* – the men that journeyed in wagon and cart from the cities a hundred years before – stretch beside the sea. No human comes this far north but for the farmer once a year, buzzing along on his quad bike as he patrols his fence line. It is land used for nothing, lying empty, carved up by lonely wire.

Dotted along the coast are the old bunkers. They are concrete and squat, built for the war that never visited the Baai, and now they look out over the empty sea. The place is devoid of man, and yet beneath the cold water there is one that adds his thinking to the ocean's song.

'*Ninety-one... Ninety-two...*'

The numbers drip through his mind.

'*Ninety-four... Ninety-five...*'

Each number wells from the one before, growing from the blue void of his thoughts as a slow leak blooms from a tap.

'*Ninety-seven...*'

Jonothan opens his eyes.

The underwater world is spread before him. Kelp stalks rise, stretching to the surface in shifting lines. *Stokvis* and *harder* flit by, unafraid of this silent man among them.

'*Ninety-nine...*' he counts within, utterly still, utterly embraced by the cold. This is his ritual, his means of surviving the past. Because every moment he feels how he abandoned her.

Each day he enters the water. Each day he dives down, finding the point where the air in his lungs crushes enough for him to attain neutral buoyancy, and each day he hangs there, calming his heart and blood so that he hovers motionless in the drifting kelp.

He focuses only on the numbers as they pass. As he goes deeper within, so the cold fades and the need to breathe, and the life of the ocean unfolds before him. His thoughts are slowing to the pace of fish. The song of all the creatures rise.

'*Eat*,' they whisper, and he glories in it. Because their song is her song.

Each day he extends his time, learning to nurse a single breath. Each day he finds further peace.

Always there is the temptation to breathe. He knows its flavour. The agony as it rises, the panic of lungs that begin to pump and strain, and then the calm that comes after, at the place where consciousness slips away. He has touched that point, and he has been lucky so far.

'*Eat*.'

He rouses himself, gliding through the kelp fields, riding the desire to breathe. Spying a likely crevice, he follows the stalk of a kelp tower down. At the bottom the cold crushes harder, holding him.

He settles before the slit in the rock. Despite the panic he glories at the quiet of his heart. He pushes his hand into the dark hole. He is numb from the cold. Sensation is blunt, a wrench instead of a scalpel, but he can still feel the hard carapace of his quarry. The eyes protrude on stalks and the feelers grow from spiny roots. He closes his fingers around the shell. He begins to pull the creature free, no matter its fighting. He kicks off, rising to the surface with the *kray* curling in his hand.

As he rises his lungs burn, but his thoughts remain calm.

'*One hundred and thirty-two...*'

He will not acknowledge the flames; he will not give in to the shameful desire that took her from him. He holds the calm of his heart, and to accentuate it he slows his rise, letting the agony build.

The shoreline is rocky, there is no beach in this windswept place. Grey clouds hang low and heavy and promise winter rain. Jonothan rises out of the foaming water and makes his way along weed-slicked rocks. He is sure-footed, sleek and shivering. Waves crash about him, but he knows their movements as he knows his own breathing; they do not assault him. His body is tempered by his months living in this wildness. Where once he was a fisher, now he has become a creature of the sea.

He climbs the rocks, approaching the bunker positioned on a promontory that looks out over the waters. Once a gun was placed here, long since removed by the distant council. What remains is a dry bunker filled with straw, a memory of their horses, and the perfect shelter for a man living wild.

Jonothan welcomes the rain. He refuses the distinction between wet and dry, between warm and cold. At night he sleeps in the open, forcing himself to embrace the night air. He clothes himself in his breathing and the passing of the stars. He has found that it is possible to ignore the cold, instead of burrowing into the straw he burrows into the heat of his own heart. And when he loses his nerve the flames of his fire bring heat to his fingers.

And always he thinks of her.

In every movement, he thinks of her.

Where is she?

Why has she not answered him?

He enters his shelter and immediately sinks to his worktop beside his fire pit. He has salvaged a discarded strip of wood from the surrounding bushes. Even here, so far from the village, there is trash to be found. Who knows what item of furniture it once was, what men once travelled here and tossed the wood away. He lifts the flapping *kray* and with a twist pulls the tail from the carapace, a mess of bowel trailing behind. He places the animal on the board and sends his blade crunching between its stalked eyes. Smoothly, he slices the shell from the tail meat and seams the tail open to remove the remaining offal. He cubes the tail in three and skewers it to three sharp cooking sticks. The head he places in a rusty tin – his cooking pot. He has found tins to be plentiful out in the bush. A morning's walk and careful looking will provide them.

He turns to the fire pit. With a twig he stirs at the dead ash that releases hidden warmth onto his palm. He plays with the sensation for a moment, his body craving it, and then he takes his hand away. He bends to blow gently on the revealed coals, and then he adds twigs from his pile of kindling and wood. A tendril of smoke begins to curl and multiply. He watches the wood fibres glow red, smoking, until suddenly there is flame. Jonothan nurtures it with his breath and then places larger sticks on top. They crackle as rain begins to fall outside. Jonothan places his cooking sticks above the flames. A fire is for cooking. Food is for nourishment. And Jonothan is for the rain. He goes out to greet it.

He squats outside his bunker. He can smell the rain as it touches the low bush spread all around. It smells of soil, and branch, and winter.

He closes his eyes, retreating into his breathing as the droplets patter onto his skin. He follows the waves of his breath, travelling down and in, away from the cold.

His mind is attuned to the stream of oxygen slipping past his nostrils. He holds a lungful and then exhales until empty, letting the silence within build until the symphony of the world becomes torrential – the patterning of the falling water, the hissing of the surf among the rocks, the sigh of the wind all around him. He sits in this place of pause and attempts to see to the other side. He has learned that every breath is a meeting with death. He waits on his empty lungs, listening to death's song, before he finally gasps and lets the air in.

He opens his eyes. The sea of low bush is bright. It stretches away ahead to the south, and to his left the east. He sees the endless fence tracking through that sea and glimpses the sand of the trail on which the farmer patrols once a year, herding his sheep. He lets his eyes wander to his right, to the north and the ocean, and his mouth falls open in astonishment.

Just beyond the rocks, riding at anchor on the autumn swell is the *Sea Queen*. The old man Mocke is at work on the deck, wrapped in orange oilskin. He flings a rubber dinghy over the side and gingerly climbs onto it.

Jonothan skips down the path to the rocky shore and dives into the surging water. The surf is rising and Mocke is precarious on his dingy. Jonothan swims hard.

The old man is methodical. He unlatches an oar and begins to paddle, swaying with the roiling surf. Jonothan reaches him. The rubber of the dinghy is hard under his freezing fingers. He catches a glimpse of the face of the old man as he loops the grab line around his wrist and turns to tow the old man to the rocks. He thinks of swimming round to the beach a kilometre distant, but it is too far. He feels a hand on his shoulder. A squeeze of recognition.

Jonothan's toe strikes rock. He stands, pulling the dinghy in closer to the first of the boulders, wanting to wedge it in so that the old man can climb out. But Mocke leaps with the swell. He lands with rubber-gripped boots and turns to help the boy drag the dinghy out of the waves.

Together they start up the bush-carpeted cliffside.

'This is a big surprise, *Oom.*' Jonothan whispers the words through his cleft lip.

As they walk Mocke is eyeing all around him. The old grey bunker perched on this wild hillside, the rain falling in mists and trails, and the shirtless man at his side, a boy no longer.

Inside the bunker the fire has died.

'Please, *Oom,*' whispers Jonothan, reaching for Mocke's oilskin and hanging it from the empty window ledge. 'Please,' he says, offering the old man his own rocky seat by the fire, squatting to remake the blaze. He offers the old man the *kray* tails, curled and hot on the sticks.

'*Dankie, seun* ... Thank you, boy.'

The *kray* head is now bright red in the cooking pot, and Jonothan hooks it off the fire and sets it at the feet of the old man.

'No, boy. You also need some hot breakfast.'

Jonothan nods in thanks. He clasps the *kray*'s head by a feeler and places it on his chopping board. With his knife he cracks the carapace and begins to pull the meat from the cavity with thumb and finger.

The two eat in silence. All the while the old man's eyes roam: the old wood used as a cutting board, the trail of soot leading to the empty window cavity, and the indent in the straw where the boy must sleep. He is living rough, and winter will only worsen.

'Where is your water?'

'I have a well, *Oom*. In the dunes. And also the rain. Can I fetch some for *Oom*?'

Mocke shakes his head, returning to the meat between his fingers. 'How long have you been at this place?'

'It is now five months, *Oom*.'

Mocke nods, eating quietly.

'It is a good place. I have food and shelter. And peace.'

'You have looked after yourself well.'

Old Mocke has finished his tail and now holds his fingers before him.

'I have no cloth here, *Oom*. I only have what I could find.'

Mocke sucks his fingers one by one and then wipes them on his trousers.

'Can I take that cup of water?'

Jonothan ducks out of the doorway, making his way quickly over the dune behind the bunker. On the other side, amidst the patterning rain and the song of the bush scent, he kneels to his well. The hole is lined with sticks and brush and the bottom is lined with loose rock. Water has pooled down there, seepage from the shallow water table, and Jonothan reaches in to scoop some of the liquid into a rusted tin can. Carefully he returns.

Inside Mocke has not moved. 'I know this place,' he says. 'I camped here as a boy. We liked to stay out for many days, tying up our dinghies beyond the swell. We fished all day, *hotnot* and *kray*, and slept in this bunker at night. Just like this. This straw even must have been the same.' He sips his water. 'But that was in summer months. This is a cold place in winter. How long will you stay?'

'I don't know, *Oom*.'

Mocke nods, allowing the silence to rest between them. He does not know this young man well. They are nearly strangers despite the years they have shared the ocean. This makes what he has to tell him all the more difficult.

'We are having good fishing in the Baai.'

'Really?'

'Yes. The foreigners have been taking big catches, our *fabrieke* cannot keep up for processing.'

'That is good.'

'Yes.'

Each listens to the crashing of the surf and the beating of his own heart. Each is waiting for the other.

'What are you doing here, *seun*? Why are you not in the Baai?'

Jonothan is careful with his answer. He considers his words, testing them against the truth of what he has found in this place, the truth of the cold who he has made his ally. 'I thought I would do like you and your friends,' he says finally, calmly. 'I would live free for a while.'

Mocke nods. He studies the young man staring resolutely at the flames. He is slight, elegant even. The brute build of his grandfather is absent. But the eyes burn with the power of that man. Mocke sighs and gathers himself.

'Jonothan,' he asks softly, 'where are your parents?'

The question catches him off-guard.

'My parents?' He turns to the old man, his face full of surprise. '*Hoekom*? – Why, *Oom*?'

'Where are they, *seun*?'

'They died, Uncle. In the war.'

Old Mocke shakes his head slowly. 'Your parents did not die in the war.'

'What does *Oom* mean? Where did they die?'

'They died very near here, in this ocean. They died with you at their side, but you were too young to remember.'

Quietly, as Jonothan watches the flickering fire, Mocke tells him the true history of his mother and father. He tells him how his mother was the daughter of a *fabriek* owner in the Baai and his father an unknown fisherman. He explains how they fled from a tyrant and how they perished. He tells the young man of the orphan that remained. And finally he tells him the name of the tyrant.

Jonothan does not speak. Only the rain patterns on the sea of bush outside, while the fire burns low.

'*Seun*? Boy?'

Jonothan shakes his head. His features are full of his mother, the dusky skin, the high cheekbones. And his father too, that strange fisher that Mocke remembers but briefly.

'Did you know him?' asks the young man finally, softly.

'I did. He fished for me.'

'What was he like?'

'He was like you, *seun*. Just like you. A gentle man. He had few words, but he could hear things that others could not. It was as if he could speak with the fishes, as if he could hear them. He was a great fisherman, like you. But you are better.'

'His face was like mine? His lip?'

'It was.'

The boy does not speak for many moments. The fire puffs out.

Both men are seeing the same image: a gentle fisher shielding his wife and son, and in the rocking of his boat he falls into the green and the water enters his boots and sucks him down. Both see how she followed him, and both now know how a child remained, and a bear.

Jonothan is so still that it unnerves the old man. Minutes pass.

'Salie was there.' The boy says this suddenly, a whisper in the rain.

'He was. He saw it all.'

'Salie showed me how to fish.'

'He did. He taught you the sea.'

'He raised me.'

The old man shakes his head sadly. 'No, boy. Nobody raised you. It is the fault of all of us. Nobody raised you.'

The boy is silent for many moments.

'Mr Mocke, where is ... my grandfather now?'

The old man places his hand on the bare skin of the boy's shoulder. Immediately he wants to pull it away, the skin is so cold.

'He is gone.'

'Gone?'

The old man tells Jonothan all of the tumultuous events since he disappeared. He tells him of the confrontation between Uncle Mike and Yoguchi, and of his bloody battle.

'I am not surprised,' says Jonothan after a time. 'He would never submit to anyone.' Jonothan turns to him and Mocke shrinks within his heart, for the young man's face has become cruel. 'And you, old man? Why have you come so far to find me? You have come to tell me this?'

'No, *seun*. I did not come to tell you this tale, even though I stand in your debt because of it. I came to make you an offer.'

'Oh?'

'Come and fish with us, with me, in the Baai. The Morkel *fabriek* stands empty, the gates are shut. It is yours. Take it and join us, and let us fish the oceans as these foreigners do. Every day Yoguchi asks for you. Join us and let *us* make terms to *him*. This way we can save our Baai.'

The boy keeps his stare trained on the old man. It is a stare the old man has seen before. It is the rage of his grandfather, the rage of Uncle Mike. But the old man presses on.

'How did you find that blue sailfish? The echo finder was not functioning.'

Jonothan smiles. A cruel smile, sharklike. 'It was luck, *Oom*. You know fishing. One day it is your day, and another it is not.'

'It was not luck. You know something of the sea that none of us know. You stand head and shoulders over us. You can save us.'

Jonothan is quiet. It seems as if he is listening. And indeed, he is.

'*Eat*,' sighs the mind of the old man. '*Eat*,' he says with fear in his eyes.

'And what do you get from it, *Oom*?'

'I get survival, my boy. A chance to fish on the sea and to eat.'

Jonothan nods. It is good that the old man tells him the truth. He squats to the little fire. He places a stick on the embers. He takes a breath, bringing himself back to the sensation of the cold running through him, his breathing. He would stop this course of hate and create his own world. He listens again to the surf and the beating of his own heart. He counts them both. He takes breath, and only when he has returned to himself does he speak.

'*Oom*. Do *you* want me to come back?'

'What do you mean now?'

Jonothan closes his eyes; the cool air slipping across his nostril is there. 'Is there any person in the Baai, fisher or line worker or even owner, that wants me back there?'

'We all do. Why do you talk like this?'

'When you were a boy, why did you and your friends come all the way out here? You can catch just as well at the Island; you can sleep on the beach there just as well.'

Mocke looks up at the younger man. Even now that the boy is calm, still Mocke finds that he is looking into the eyes of Uncle Mike.

'Well?'

'What are you asking, *seun*?'

'Why did you come out here, *Oom*, with your friends, when you were a boy like me?'

'We came for friendship.'

The boy nods.

'Yes. Friendship. I lived in the Baai all my life. I have worked for the Baai since I can remember, and I have not one friend in that place.'

'Jonny, the past is done. Don't take the path of bitterness. That was your grandfather's path.'

'I don't want to take that path, you are right. Tell me, did my grandfather ever speak of me?'

Mocke sighs. He looks to his hands and then back to the boy's flashing eyes.

'Your grandfather was a difficult man. I think none of us of the Baai could understand him. He came from a different place. He knew war before he knew peace.'

'Did he ever speak of me?'

'He looked out for you as best he could. I believe it was always his wish to have you take over the Morkel *fabriek*.'

'Did he ever speak to you of me?'

Mocke looks down. He cannot hold the eyes of the boy any longer. 'No,' he admits, shaking his head. Once again rain begins to wet the veld outside.

'Old man, you are a good servant of your village. You were always kind to me.' He turns to reach for Mocke's oilskin. He hands it to him. 'Thank you for coming to find me. I will consider what you have said. If I come to you, it will be for you and not for the Baai, and it will be five days from today.'

Mocke raises his hand, palm up to the boy. He wants to say something more, his heart is heavy, but all has been said. 'Okay, Jonny. That sounds like a good plan.'

The boy takes the hand and helps old Mocke to rise.

'Thank you.'

The sensation of the boy's strong grip stays with him as Mocke makes his way back to the *Sea Queen*.

'Five days, *Oom*,' says Jonothan, looking up to the old man from the cold, grey water.

'I hope so,' mutters the old man as he waves the young one goodbye.

In the wet weather, among the grey cloud hanging low, while Jonothan swims back to the turbulent shore, Mocke unhitches his anchor line. Hand over hand, he pulls that grim iron up through the cold.

That night Jonothan lies uncovered on the beach, his eyes towards the heavens. The rain has passed and there is a break in the cloud overhead. Up there, in the winter sky, the hunter Orion is gone for the season. It is only when heat returns that he will return also. Now the scorpion rides high. He turns to the Southern Cross. He follows its length to meet the trail set out by the pointers and drops his eyes to the horizon. South. The direction of the Island, and beyond that the Baai.

He turns in the dark, looking to the north, and then to the west.

'*Where are you?*'

There is no answer but for the wind and the booming surf.

'*Will I see you again?*'

Neither the surf nor the wind reply.

He places his hands beside him, his palms flat on the cold sand. He glories in each grain that rubs against his skin.

'*Are you there?*' he asks of the wet sand. '*Are you there?*' he asks of the world, and nothing but the wind sighs across the lonely beach. He places his hands over the hole in his stomach, the place from where his longing goes out to her. He holds the wound, trying to seal it.

He sleeps this night as he has slept many others, looking up to the stars as they sail by, sleeping and waking from the cold, sleeping and waking, until, finally, dawn.

In the coming sun he knows what he must do. He stands stiffly and begins to run.

Four nights later the sky is dark and heavy, and beneath it the Baai slumbers. None are awake but old Mocke, who waits with a lone light burning in his *fabriek*. This coming morning is the day the boy will come, if he comes, and he hopes it will be so. The old man sits quietly, waiting out the night, full of all that has come to pass. The Baai he has known these long years, since his own first memory, the Baai of his father and his grandfather, seems changed forever, stained by the foreigner's ships.

'Nothing will ever be the same,' the old man mutters, knowing it was always so. Nothing ever was the same, but for the roiling of the world, moving to and fro. He is an old resident, a long seer of the tides and seasons and decades, of the families that have come and gone. He has seen it all and he knows it still – to him there is only one thing that truly matters: to eat. And so he hopes that the boy will come to him, so that he and his own may eat, yet he knows that it may not be so.

Beneath the same dark and heavy cloud, the boy stands on a beach looking out toward the rocks of the Island a kilometre from the shore. They are hidden in the darkness, but he knows they are there.

'*My love?*'

He steps into the water, wading deeper, and then sinks his face beneath.

'*Where are you?*'

He swims out to the Sentinel, effortlessly gliding through the cold, knowing all the fishers from the Baai are not yet on the sea. He enters the northern channel, his body still strong, and comes to rest at the base of the rising tower, bobbing before it. He puts his forehead to the rock.

'My love?'

He dives under, using the rock to pull him down. With fresh lungs he finds the entrance to her cave and pulls himself inward. He enters the chamber and pauses in the soft moonlight cast through the flume. The walls that he knows so well rise up around him, riven with the marks of drills. Men have scoured the rock deeply. The clams that once gilded this place are stripped from every surface. There is nothing here but scars.

He understands. The violation is complete. He remembers her face when she saw Uncle Mike at his hut, on the morning that they came down from the mountain, and his final glimpse of her through the clouds of the dark one's ink. Cruelty is alien to her, and greed is more than she can bear. He knows now why she is gone. He rides the need to breathe, letting it light up his eyes before he kicks his way out of the cave and up to the surface.

The light is building now. It will not be long until the Baai's first fishers arrive with their nets ready. He treads water, at one with the cold and all the creatures within it. He finds Venus, fading to morning's light. He bids her goodbye.

He sinks down.

He hangs for what seems an age, the desire to breathe slipping further and further away. He merges with the water, the quality of his sight shifting to that of a fish. He looks ahead of him, out to the great drop-off where the shelf of the continent sails down. He looks above him to where the sun is rising orange above the veil. And there he sees a rainbow fish. Its colours shimmer as it drifts above the mighty void, tracing lazy circles, until finally it swims off.

Jonothan watches its going, a stray bubble escaping his blueing lips. He waits one moment more, and then he kicks out with hands and feet and slides after it, into the void, the shelf dropping away beneath him.

ABOUT THE AUTHOR

Milton Schorr was born in 1981 in Cape Town, South Africa. He attended the University of Cape Town as a student of theatre, thereafter creating theatre works across South Africa. As a writer and actor he has received the Imbewu Scriptwriting award for his play *The Heroin Diaries*, and both the 'IDIDTHAT Best of Reel for Direction Craft' and 'Vimeo Staff Pick' award for his short film *Surrender*, and has appeared in blockbuster film productions such as *Resident Evil: The Final Chapter, Outlander, Tomb Raider,* and *Redeeming Love*. He is a renowned travel and sports writer, with credits in many of South Africa's major publications. His work can be seen at miltonschorr.co.za. *Strange Fish* is his first novel.

COMING SOON – 'A Man Of The Road' by Milton Schorr

Author and actor Milton Schorr's second novel, *A Man Of The Road*, tells the story of Little Mikey, a young boy from the mythical West Coast town of Freeburg, who must one day set out on an epic cross-country hitch-hiking journey. On his dangerous way he encounters characters from all sections of South African society, and learns what it is to be 'a man of the road.' The novel is based on Milton Schorr's years of experience hitch-hiking the roads of Southern Africa, Germany and Australia, and will be available worldwide in early 2022.

COMING SOON – 'Strange Fish' 2 & 3

The tale of *Strange Fish* is not complete. 'I wrote what I thought was a third act for *Strange Fish* during July of 2020,' says author Milton Schorr. 'Eventually I realised that what I thought was the third act must in fact be the third part of a trilogy. This means that *Strange Fish* Part Three is largely already written, while *Strange Fish* Part Two is yet to be put to paper. I plan to do this during 2022.' Look out for *Strange Fish* 2 & 3 in 2023.

Find Out More:

To stay abreast of Milton Schorr's coming works, tours and author activities, visit **www.pilgrimspressbooks.com** or follow us on social media at **@pilgrimspressbooks.com.** Alternatively, scan the QR Code to the right by simply pointing your camera phone at it and hitting the link that appears.

'Strange Fish' Is Available As An Audiobook!

Strange Fish has partnered with BiB, Africa's online audiobook platform, bringing Africa's beautiful stories to the world. Download the BiB app to your phone or computer by visiting **https://qrco.de/bblj4C** and following the prompts to *Strange Fish.* Alternatively, scan the QR Code to the right by pointing your camera phone at it and hitting the link that appears.